It was her.

The woman who was his destiny. But it couldn't be. He went to the bed and stood staring down at her. With a gentle hand, he pushed her tousled curls away from her face.

Rory opened her midnight blue eyes and looked straight at Daniel. More asleep than not, she took his hand in hers and held it against her cheek. The tiniest of smiles touched her lips as she closed her eyes and went back to sleep.

Daniel didn't try to take his hand away and simply left it in hers as he sat on the edge of the bed.

His grandfather had been right. He recognized her.

And even as he gazed upon the face of the woman he'd carried in his heart for twenty-five years, there was a terrible reality with which he had to deal.

His love was also his enemy.

How had this happened?

Dear Reader,

Book #1000?! In February, 1982, when Silhouette Special Edition was first published, that seemed a far distant goal. And now, almost fourteen years later, here we are!

We're opening CELEBRATION 1000 with a terrific book from the beloved Diana Palmer—*Maggie's Dad*. Diana was one of the first authors to contribute to Special Edition, and now she's returned with this tender tale of love reborn.

Lindsay McKenna continues her action-packed new series, MORGAN'S MERCENARIES: LOVE AND DANGER. The party goes on with *Logan's Bride* by Christine Flynn— the first HOLIDAY ELOPEMENTS, three tales of love and weddings over the holiday season. And join the festivities with wonderful stories by Jennifer Mikels, Celeste Hamilton and Brittany Young.

We have so many people to thank for helping us to reach this milestone. Silhouette Special Edition would not be what it is today without our marvelous writers. I want to take a moment, though, to mention one author—Sondra Stanford. She gave us Book #7, *Silver Mist*, and many other wonderful stories. We lost her in October 1991 after a valiant struggle against cancer. We miss her; she brought a great deal of happiness to all who knew her.

And our very special thanks to our readers. Your imaginations and brave hearts allow books to take flight— and all of us can never thank you enough for that!

The celebration continues in December and January—with books by Nora Roberts, Debbie Macomber, Sherryl Woods and many more of your favorite writers! Happy Book 1000—to each and every romantic!

Sincerely,

Tara Gavin, Senior Editor

Please address questions and book requests to:
Silhouette Reader Service
U.S.: 3010 Walden Ave., P.O. Box 1325, Buffalo, NY 14269
Canadian: P.O. Box 609, Fort Erie, Ont. L2A 5X3

BRITTANY YOUNG
BRAVE HEART

SPECIAL EDITION®

Published by Silhouette Books
America's Publisher of Contemporary Romance

This book is dedicated to my parents, Robert and Helen Harrisson, with heartfelt thanks to them for introducing me to the reservations of northern Wisconsin and for their patience with me while I explored.

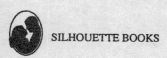 SILHOUETTE BOOKS

ISBN 0-373-09996-7

BRAVE HEART

Copyright © 1995 by Brittany Young

This edition published by arrangement with Harlequin Books S.A.

® and TM are trademarks of Harlequin Books S.A., used under license. Trademarks indicated with ® are registered in the United States Patent and Trademark Office, the Canadian Trade Marks Office and in other countries.

Printed in U.S.A.

Books by Brittany Young

BRITTANY YOUNG

lives and writes in Racine, Wisconsin. She has traveled to most of the countries that serve as the settings for her books and finds the research into the language, customs, history and literature of these countries among the most demanding and rewarding aspects of her writing.

Dear Reader,

As one of Silhouette's original authors, having begun writing for the Romance line in 1980, it's a privilege for me to be part of the celebration of the publication of Silhouette Special Edition's 1000th novel. My first Special Edition was published less than a year ago, and I hope to write many more. These books touch my heart when I write them and when I read them. They're truly romantic, with characters that still value qualities such as honor, loyalty, integrity and fidelity. Throughout the books, we have the pleasure——at times bittersweet——of watching our heroes and heroines falling more and more deeply in love. And when they do finally share themselves completely, they don't have sex; they make warm, passionate love. We know that this man and this woman are meant to be together forever. Sigh...

Both readers and writers of Special Edition novels have Senior Editor Tara Gavin to thank for her steady guiding hand and intrinsic understanding of the magic that is romance.

Prologue

*Whispering Pines Indian Reservation
in Northern Wisconsin*

This night on the reservation was dark and hushed. Deep in the forested hills sacred to the tribe, there was a clearing where a fire burned, sending sparks snapping high into the air. An old Indian man, his leathery dark face deeply lined, his brown eyes weary, sat cross-legged on the ground and stared at the flames.

A seven-year-old boy sat beside him, as still as the night, his black, shiny hair hanging straight to the middle of his back, his dark brown eyes more serious than any child's should have been. He sat tall and erect, his lithe body already showing signs of the lean muscularity he would have as a man.

A log fell into the fire and hissed. Flames flashed momentarily higher and sent sparks into the air. The boy's smooth skin glowed a bronze color.

"A girl-child was born this night," said the old man in his native tongue.

"She is the other half of you." He looked into the intelligent eyes of his cherished grandson. "She will come to you unexpectedly one day, Daniel."

"How will I know her, Grandfather?"

"Your heart will recognize her, as hers will recognize you." He looked into the flames again. "There will be many problems to overcome, perhaps more than either of you will be able to deal with. Difficult choices will have to be made by both of you."

He turned his head to look at the child. "Daniel, you must never forget where you come from. You must place your heritage and your people above any other consideration, including your own happiness. You, by virtue of your birth, are the hope for the future."

"I understand, Grandfather."

Ten years later
Whispering Pines Indian Reservation

Seventeen-year-old Daniel Blackhawk had felt hauntingly troubled for days. He had no idea why. But no matter what he did, the feeling wouldn't go away.

As he sat reading in the log home where he lived with his grandfather, he suddenly closed his book and looked at the ageless man seated across the table. He needed to go into the hills to think.

Gray Cloud, as always, seemed to understand. With no words spoken, he inclined his head as though giving permission.

Daniel brought nothing with him as he began a journey that would take him eight hours on foot to complete. He loved to run, and he ran now, shirtless and with a silent grace that befitted a boy who had grown up so close to nature. A wolf who had been his constant companion since childhood ran with him.

When he got to the sacred hills, he climbed them effortlessly, moving through virgin forest whose every tree he knew by heart. As a child, he had come here often with his grandfather.

By the time he'd climbed to the top of the highest hill, it was night. Daniel went to a stream and cupped his hands in the rapidly running water to capture a drink, then sat a few yards from the stream, his body spotlighted by the moon. He pushed his long hair out of his face with a still-wet hand. The wolf sat nearby, watching, alert to any sound that didn't belong there.

In a few days Daniel would be leaving the reservation for the university. It would be a long time before he was able to return. Funds were in short supply. His scholarships were a tremendous help, but he was going to have to work to pay his living expenses.

He would miss this place.

But even as he had that thought, he realized it wasn't that which had been troubling him.

It was the girl.

As clearly as Daniel knew she was out there somewhere, he knew something terrible had happened in her life. It was as though her spirit were calling to his for help, for comfort.

Tilting his face toward the star-filled sky, Daniel closed his eyes and focused his thoughts on her completely, sending her a part of himself, letting her know she wasn't alone.

Suburban Chicago

Wearing a dark blue dress and with her long, curly, coppery hair held neatly away from her face with a dark blue ribbon, ten-year-old Rory Milbourne sat alone on the couch in the elegant living room of her uncle's home. There were more than a hundred people present, most of them clustered together in small groups. Some treated the evening as a social event, talking and laughing.

Others took discreetly sympathetic looks at her and whispered to each other. Every once in a while someone would walk over to Rory and squeeze her shoulder, with a kind of gentle understanding that was intended as comfort.

She had buried her parents that afternoon.

Now she was in a home that wasn't hers, forever after to be living with a widowed uncle she barely knew and a cousin she didn't like and who most certainly didn't like her.

And so she sat, dry-eyed, expressionless—lost.

Her cousin Bruce, tall for twelve and slightly overweight, stood in front of her. Finally, he spoke, "I don't want you here."

She met his look with a direct one of her own. "I know," she said quietly.

"Nobody wants you here. My dad is just being nice."

Rory was silent. What could she say?

"I'm gonna warn you right now that while you're here, and it probably won't be for long, I don't want you touching any of my stuff or talking to my friends. Okay?"

She still didn't say anything.

Bruce pinched her arm.

"Stop that!" said Rory, as she pulled her arm away from him and rubbed the sore spot.

"Then answer me."

"Okay," she said. "I won't do any of those things."

Feeling satisfied that he'd set the ground rules, Bruce walked away from her.

Her uncle, a basically kind man, sat beside her on the couch and took her hand in his. "How are you doing, Rory?"

"Fine," she lied.

"I'm glad to see that you and Bruce are becoming friends. Think of him the way you would a big brother. And though I know I can never replace your mom and dad in your heart, I hope that you'll grow to think of me as more than just your guardian." He smiled at her. "Quite honestly, I've always wanted a daughter and I can't think of anyone I'd rather have fill that role than you."

Rory managed a hint of a smile. "Thank you."

"I love you already. Maybe someday you'll come to love me, as well."

Rory nodded.

"And remember, dear, that if you need someone to talk to, I'm here for you."

"Thank you, Uncle Bill."

Bill Milbourne had never been very good with children. He felt awkward around them—even his own son. And with Rory, well, he didn't feel as though he were getting through to her. She was making all of the correct responses, but he sensed a barrier of some kind between them. Of course, she was a ten-year-old who had just lost her parents and her home. Perhaps now wasn't the time for a pep talk. He clumsily squeezed her fingers and rose from the couch.

Rory stayed where she was for a while, watching those around her with haunted midnight blue eyes.

She felt numb.

People came and went throughout the evening. She accepted their pats and sympathetic murmurings for as long as she could bear to, but there came a point when she had to get away from everyone.

Her uncle watched with concern as Rory walked to the patio doors and went outside. When her uncle would have gone after her, a woman friend of his lightly touched his arm and shook her head. "Let her have some time alone,'' she said softly. ''Maybe that's what she needs.''

Rory walked away from the house, out of the light that spilled from the windows. Halfway across the manicured lawn, she stopped and sat on the grass.

For a long time, she stared blankly into the night. She didn't know what to think or feel. She just knew she missed her mom and dad so much that her entire body ached.

Silent tears filled her eyes and spilled onto her cheeks. Anyone looking at her from behind wouldn't have known from her straight little back and shoulders that she was crying. She made no sound. Her pain was hers alone.

Once the tears began to fall, Rory couldn't stop them. She didn't even try. They rolled down her cheeks and dropped onto her dress. She didn't bother to wipe them away.

She sat like that for a long time, unaware of her uncle's worried glances out the window.

Finally Rory lay back on the grass and stared at the sky. The tears that were left dropped from the corners of her eyes and into her hair.

Slowly her bleary gaze focused on the sky, bright with stars, seeming to twinkle more than they usually did because she was seeing them through the prisms of teardrops. She took a deep, tremulous breath that failed to ease the tightness in her chest.

The despair she felt was almost overwhelming. Her parents were gone. She would never see them again.

A single star shot across the sky. Rory watched until it disappeared from sight.

She wiped the backs of her hands across her cheeks and continued looking at the night sky.

The terrible ache in her chest gradually began to ease. She could breathe without it hurting so much.

As her despair lifted, it was replaced with a warm serenity that enveloped her like an embrace.

Rory continued to look at the stars, compelled by some force she didn't understand, until exhaustion overtook her. Her eyelids grew heavier and heavier until finally, for the first time since her parents died, she drifted into a sleep so soothing and deep that she didn't wake when her uncle lifted her in his arms and carried her to her new room.

Chapter One

Fifteen years later
Chicago

Rory walked into her uncle's outer office carrying an airline suit bag and a briefcase. "Hi, Mary," she said with a tired smile to the secretary. "Is my uncle in?"

"He's in his office having lunch."

Rory looked at the expensive watch on her wrist. "Lunch? It's past three."

"It's been a very long afternoon," said Mary meaningfully.

"Problems?"

"Just one, but it's big. Whispering Pines Reservation."

"What's wrong?"

Mary walked around the desk and took the suit bag from her. "I'll hang this up for you. It appears the tribe is protesting our corporate right to mine for copper on the reservation."

"But we have governmental permission."

"According to them, the United States government has no right to set foot on their land, much less move in mining equipment."

"First of all, it's not 'their' land. It's government property. The tribe has been allowed to use the land, but they certainly don't own it."

"All I know is that Bruce has been at the reservation for the past week unsuccessfully trying to get things rolling. He came back this morning and said that it doesn't look good."

"So what do we do now?"

Mary shrugged. "You'll have to talk to your uncle. I don't understand the finer points of what's going on. And you'd better let Bruce know you're back before you go into your uncle's office. He's been buzzing me for the past two hours to see if you'd arrived."

"Thanks, Mary."

"Can I get you something to eat?"

"No," said Rory over her shoulder. "I'll just nibble on my uncle's leftovers."

As she opened the door of her cousin's office, she started to say something, but he shushed her with an impatient gesture of his hand and pointed at the telephone. Rory heard someone's voice at the other end of the line as it came through the speakerphone. "So when exactly do you want me to set the—"

Bruce grabbed the handset and turned off the speaker. "Excuse me, my cousin just walked into my office." He watched as Rory sat down across from him. "And in answer to your question," he continued, "I think you should set things in motion tonight. The sooner we can put an end to this the better."

Bruce was silent while he listened to the other man speak.

"Hold off on any further negotiations until you hear from me," he said finally. "In the meantime, I'll send you that packet of information I promised."

As Bruce hung up, he looked at his watch and then at Rory. "You're late." It was more of an accusation than a comment.

"My plane was delayed."

"Then you should have called."

Rory ignored his remark. She worked for her uncle, not Bruce. "What's so urgent?"

"We have problems on the Whispering Pines Reservation project."

"Mary just told me."

"You prepared some of the paperwork for it."

"That's right."

"While you were doing the research, did you come across anything that would give the government the right to evict the tribe from the reservation?"

"No. But by the same token, I didn't come across anything that said it couldn't be done."

"That's good." He nodded as he got out of his chair and walked around his desk to the door. "Come on. Dad wanted to talk to you as soon as you came in."

Rory followed her cousin out into the firm's hallways. Their offices were arranged in a circle, leading from Mary's office. Most of the offices of the other corporate employees were arranged similarly and spread out on the tenth floor of the building.

Bruce knocked on his father's door.

"Come in."

When they walked in, Bill Milbourne smiled at his niece. "Rory, you're looking lovely, as always."

And she did, in her slim-fitting suit and high heels. She was the picture of dignity except for the loopy curls of her shoulder-length coppery hair. She'd given up trying to tame it years ago.

"Thank you."

"Well, don't leave me in suspense. What happened?"

"I bought the building and the grounds."

"As per our initial offer?"

"I had to make a few concessions about when they vacate the building and what they can take when they go but, bottom line, it's yours."

Bill Milbourne leaned back in his chair with a satisfied smile. He hadn't doubted for a moment that his niece would come through for him. She always did. "You see, Bruce," he said to his son, "it pays to have an attorney in the family. That's why I want her on this other project."

"Whispering Pines?" asked Rory. She lifted half an egg roll from her uncle's plate and perched gracefully on the arm of his chair.

"I see you've heard."

"From the moment I got here."

Bruce sat in a chair across from his father.

"We've got big problems," said her uncle. "I hired a Wisconsin mining company for the job. They have the men and the equipment on the reservation, ready to go to work, and suddenly everything is at a standstill. Tribal protestors are blocking the machinery with their cars and won't budge."

"We have a legal right to be there," said Rory. "Have them arrested."

"Bruce and I discussed that, and frankly it's not really a viable solution to the problem. At least not at this point. The last thing we want to do is antagonize them unnecessarily and bring bad publicity raining down on us."

"So what are you going to do? Take them to court?"

"If I have to, but again, not yet. You know as well as I do that a court action of this magnitude might take years to be heard. I don't have years. At the moment I'm about as financially strapped as I've ever been. You and Bruce are both aware of some of the bad investments I've made."

"How strapped are we talking about?" she asked.

Bill Milbourne looked at his niece with worried gray eyes. "I could lose it all. Everything I've spent my life trying to build."

Rory was shocked. "I had no idea you were in this kind of trouble. Why didn't you say something sooner?"

"Frankly, I thought it was just a run of bad luck that wouldn't last." He shrugged. "I was wrong. This mining deal is make-it-or-break-it time for me. Over the past I've sunk a fortune into surveys that show over and over again that the hills on that reservation are rich with copper. The legal work is done, the men have been hired and the equipment has been purchased. We extract the copper, sell it, turn over a portion of our profits to the government and keep the rest for ourselves. I can't afford to have millions of dollars worth of machinery and manpower sitting idle waiting for a bunch of hotheads to come to their senses."

"And we don't have time to wade through governmental red tape," added Bruce.

"So where do I fit in to all of this?" she asked.

"You, my dear, are our trump card. You're familiar with certain legal aspects of this matter and you're a good negotiator. I want you to go to the reservation and use all of your charm and skill to negotiate an end to this standoff."

"What am I negotiating with?"

"Money. Right now, since they don't technically own the land, the tribe hasn't been offered a percentage of what's taken out. I think this could be the answer to our problem."

"Have you approached them with this?"

"No. I was trying to avoid having to give them anything."

"Let's face it," said Bruce, "they aren't taking on any of the financial risk of this venture. All they have to do is sit back and watch us do the work."

"That's right," said her uncle. "But I've reached a point where, even though I don't think they deserve it, I'm willing to share a certain amount of my profits with them just to keep them quiet."

"And you think this will work?"

"Money talks every time."

"Is there a particular group leading the protests?" she asked.

"Not really," said Bruce. "But there is a man who seems to orchestrate matters."

"Is he a member of the tribe?"

"His name is Blackhawk. Daniel Blackhawk."

"Where does he get his authority?"

"His grandfather, an old man named Gray Cloud, is—I guess you'd call him a wise man or medicine man, or some nonsense like that. He's revered by the members of the tribe. I guess because Blackhawk is his grandson, they do whatever he tells them to."

"And right now he's telling them that the land should be left the way it is," said her uncle. "I personally think if we can get Gray Cloud and Blackhawk on our side, the others will come around to our way of thinking in short order."

"So what you're saying is that you think these two men can be bought?"

"Exactly. And that's where you come in."

"Negotiation," she said.

"You're good at it. There's no one else I trust more than you when it comes to getting me what I want. You haven't blown a deal yet."

Rory turned her head to gaze out the window for a moment. "Have you thought about what you'll do if they don't agree to your money-for-land deal?"

"They will," said her uncle. "You should see this place. There isn't even a decent road running through it. They need the money."

"But what if?"

"I don't even want to consider the possibility at this point. And you shouldn't, either."

Rory didn't like not having options. It didn't give her any room for maneuvering. Up to this point, she'd always been able to threaten to back out of a deal if it wasn't going the way she wanted. That wasn't possible here.

"I want you to go to Whispering Pines Reservation without warning anyone that you're coming," said her uncle. "Catching people off guard is always better than letting them make plans. When you get there, make a quick visit to the mining site so you can get a feel for what's at stake, then get in touch with both Blackhawk and Gray Cloud. Talk to them. Reason with them. Do whatever it takes to end this impasse, so we can get to work."

"I'll be there on and off to give you whatever backup support you need," said Bruce.

"But you're in charge, Rory," said her uncle. "Make no mistake, this is going to be a delicate balancing act, and you'll need to be able to make your own calls. About the only thing you can't do is offer them any percentage over what we agree to now.''

Rory didn't feel good about this. She had a niggling feeling of something not being quite right.

"So?" her uncle asked. "Will you help me out of this mess I've gotten myself into?"

Rory smiled fondly at him. How could she refuse a request like that? "I'll do my best."

"Good girl."

Rory would have done almost anything for her uncle. He had been her biggest supporter and noisiest cheerleader for the past fifteen years of her life. She had grown to love him as though he were her real father. "When do you want me to go?"

"Tomorrow, first thing."

Rory picked up a napkin and wiped her fingers. "All right. I'd better do some homework."

The older man tapped his pen on the desk. "Look, Rory, the thing you need to pound home with those people is that I'm doing them a big favor by choosing their land to mine. All they have to do is cooperate and I'll make us all rich."

She rose from the arm of his chair. "Is there anything I need to know before I go?"

"Just go through the files. The more you know about what's already gone on, the better off you'll be."

"All right." She leaned over and kissed his forehead. "I'll talk to you later."

When she'd gone, Bruce turned to his father. "Do you think you're making a mistake in sending her?"

"I wouldn't have asked her if I didn't think she could handle it."

"And what if this turns out to be the one she loses?"

"Then we'll try something else."

Rory, unaware of the conversation going on behind the door she'd just closed, stepped into the outer office. "Mary, would you please pull the file on the Whispering Pines Reservation?"

Mary pointed to the corner of her desk where a six-inch-thick file was taking up space. "I'm way ahead of you."

"Thanks," she said. She scooped it up and started paging through the file as she walked. "And book me on a flight to..." She turned to look at Mary. "What's near the reservation?"

"Nothing."

"Well, get me as close as you can and arrange a rental car."

"Any particular type?"

"Something comfortable. I'll probably be doing a lot of driving."

"Gotcha."

Rory went into her office and closed the door, then opened it again. "And make sure it has a phone."

"No problem."

She closed the door again. With a tired sigh, she stepped out of her high heels, walked around her desk to her chair and pulled the file toward her. She had a lot of reading to do in very little time.

"You're restless tonight," said Daniel's grandfather from the rocking chair on the porch of his tiny home. Since Daniel's childhood, it had been almost a daily ritual for him and Gray Cloud to end the day together.

"I know. It's something in the air."

"It's something inside you, Daniel, not the air. It's time for you to think about settling down and starting a family."

"Not yet."

The old man rose and put his hand on Daniel's shoulder. "Soon."

Daniel covered his grandfather's hand with his own.

"It's late," Gray Cloud said. "Too late for old men to be awake. Good night, Daniel."

"Good night, Grandfather."

As Gray Cloud went to his door, he stopped suddenly, eyes closed, face raised to the sky. "Do you smell that?" he asked.

Daniel took a deep breath. "Smoke."

Gray Cloud pointed south. "It's coming from that direction."

Daniel took off running down a path that wound through the woods, dodging low-hanging branches illuminated by the full moon. The smell of smoke grew stronger with each passing moment. And then he saw the flames shooting high into the air.

When he got to a clearing in the woods, he saw the burning house. He grabbed two buckets and joined the half a dozen other people already there, filling containers with lake water, running the twenty yards back to the house and throwing it on the fire again and again and again.

It was hopeless, but that didn't stop people from trying.

"Where's the fire truck?" yelled Daniel over the noise of voices and the crackle of burning wood as he emptied his buckets.

"Broken," someone yelled back.

Daniel set his buckets down long enough to strip off his shirt and toss it aside. He labored with the others for nearly an hour until there wasn't a muscle in his body that didn't ache. For a time they seemed to be making progress against the tenacity of the flames, but it turned out to be a momentary lull. Something inside exploded and within seconds the entire home was engulfed.

Glistening with perspiration, Daniel stood back with the others, his bare torso blackened by soot, and watched as the roof collapsed with a whoosh, sending flaming debris shooting everywhere.

A young man and woman, their arms around each other, stood next to him and gazed silently at the blaze as everything they owned was destroyed.

"I'm so sorry," said Daniel. "How did this happen?"

"I don't know," said the man, clearly bewildered. "We'd already put the kids to bed and were about to turn in ourselves when our dog started barking and wouldn't stop. I went to check and found the fire on the front porch. I tried to beat it out with a blanket, but it was too late. It was all I could do to get my family out before it spread.''

''You and your family are welcome to stay at my home until you can rebuild.''

''Thank you, Daniel, but we're going to my sister's house in town for now.''

The woman wiped tears from her cheeks with her fingertips. ''Everything is gone.'' Her voice was little more than a whisper. ''The things given to me by my grandmother, pictures of our children...everything.''

The man pulled his wife closer to his side. ''But we're all alive and unharmed. Let's be grateful for that.''

She nodded. ''Let's go,'' said the woman to her husband. ''I'm exhausted.''

As they walked away, Daniel continued to look at the fire.

A man in the uniform of the tribal police walked around the cabin and stopped next to Daniel. ''What do you think? Arson?''

''You know it is, Jake. You can still smell the gasoline.''

''Did you say anything to them?'' he asked, inclining his head toward the man and woman getting into their car.

''No. There's no sense in frightening people unnecessarily.''

"Meaning what? You think it's Milbourne?"

Daniel didn't say anything for a moment. "Yes."

"He left town yesterday."

"I'm not saying he set it himself. My guess is that he hired someone to do it for him."

"One of the mining crew?"

"It's possible. Or maybe one of us. It would have to be a person who can find his way around without being seen—or if he's seen, not be noticed."

Jake, who had been a good friend of Daniel's since childhood, nodded. "That makes sense. I called the city. They'll be sending an investigator first thing tomorrow morning."

"For all the good that'll do."

"They can tell us how and where it started even if they can't tell us who."

"I suppose." Daniel looked silently at the smoldering remains of the house. He had a bad feeling about this. A feeling that this wasn't going to be the last fire.

Jake slapped him on the shoulder. "Go on home, Daniel. There's nothing more you can do here. And don't try to take on the Milbourne family yourself. That's my job."

Daniel looked at Jake, then turned away from his friend and headed into the woods. At first his steps were slow and tired as he walked down the path along the lake that led to his own home. A wolf, the third generation of the one who'd followed him as a child, had been watching from the woods and now trotted beside him. As Daniel's pace picked up, so did the wolf's. After a time, the animal left the human path to follow one of his own.

Daniel gradually picked up speed until he broke into a run. He ran full-out, as he always did, pushing himself. A startled deer ran into the woods in a flurry of hoofbeats.

As Daniel approached the log cabin he'd built with his own hands, he veered off the path and dove into the cold lake to swim the final mile with long, smooth strokes. Climbing onto the embankment, he gave a single shake of his head that sent his long hair flying and a spray of water shooting into the air. His chest rose and fell with his deep breaths.

If he ever found out with any certainty that Milbourne was behind the fire, nothing would save him. Daniel took care of his own.

Rory sat straight up in bed. Her heart pounded as though she'd been running.

She pushed her hair away from her face, damp with perspiration, and tried to focus in the dark room. Her heart calmed a little, but she was still too nervous to relax. Getting up, she walked to the window and pulled the drape aside so she could look out. A full moon glowed above the tall buildings across the street from her apartment.

Ever since she could remember, the night sky had had a calming effect on her. Tonight was the same.

Sitting on the window seat, she wrapped her arms around her legs and rested her cheek on her knees. Her dream gradually took form in her conscious mind. It was the same dream she'd had for years. She was lost and desperately trying to find her way home. Then she saw a man—at least she saw the shadow of a man—beckoning to her. She knew if she could just get to him that everything would be all right. She tried to run to him, but her legs wouldn't move. It was as though they were weighted with lead. Helplessly she watched as he faded away. She felt a desperation unlike any she'd ever felt before, an ache that started in her heart and spread through her body.

She knew it was just a dream. It wasn't even a particularly bad dream. It was the way it made her feel that frightened her.

But there was something else about the dream that haunted her.

Who was the man? She felt compelled to find the answer.

But how?

Would she ever know?

Chapter Two

Rory looked at the countryside as she drove down the old two-lane highway. It was late summer. The corn growing in the rich, dark soil was tall and nearly ready to harvest. Neat white farmhouses, red barns and giant silos dotted the land. Herds of black-and-white cows grouped in pastures drowsily chewed, oblivious to passing traffic.

It smelled earthy and clean.

But it was definitely in the middle of nowhere. A nice place to visit, but Rory couldn't imagine living there.

The drive from the airport seemed to go on and on. Too long. As she passed through a small town that didn't consist of much more than a gas station and some rough-looking bars, Rory picked up the map from the seat beside her and glanced at it. It seemed odd that there had been no signs or any other indication that the reservation was only ten miles away, but she was indeed headed in the right direction.

As she left the town, she once again picked up speed. The pastures and fields were turning into thick forests that seemed to grow thicker the closer she came to the reservation.

Rory was about to check her map again when a simple sign appeared announcing that the next turn led to the Whispering Pines Reservation. Finally, she thought, as she took it and found herself on a narrow dirt road enclosed by forest on either side. Clouds of dust rolled off her tires and filled the air behind her.

She drove for miles without seeing any signs of life: no people, no cars, no homes. Where was everyone?

She finally came across a log cabin with a sign announcing that it was a general store. She parked next to the only car in front of it, a battered old pickup truck, and looked around. It seemed deserted.

Feeling out of place and oddly vulnerable, she climbed from the car, made her way up the steps and through the creaky screen door. A woman standing behind the counter smiled at her. Rory smiled back.

Feeling as though she should buy something before asking for information, her high heels tapped the worn wood floor as she walked through the store looking at the shelves of food, pots and pans, rolling pins and postcards. She chose a few cards and a can of soda and carried them to the front. ''Is there a hotel anywhere near here?'' asked Rory, as the woman added up her purchases.

"No. Not on the reservation. There's a motel about fifteen miles from here. It's not fancy," she said with a polite eye on Rory's expensive suit, "but it's clean. Would you like directions?"

"Yes, thank you." Rory handed her some money. "Could you also tell me where I can find the hills?"

The woman looked at her curiously. The hills were sacred to her people. What would a white woman want with them?

Rory thought she'd used the wrong term, so she tried again. "What I'm looking for is the area of the reservation that's been zoned for copper mining?"

The woman's friendliness was replaced with hostility.

Rory knew instantly that she'd made a mistake and she tried to correct it. "I'm not here to cause trouble," she said with a reassuring smile. "I just want to talk to the people involved."

The woman looked at her for a long moment. "I'll have to draw you a map." There was no return smile.

"Thank you."

Rory listened while the woman explained the turns she needed to make, sketching them on the back of the small brown bag she'd put the postcards in.

"I appreciate your help."

The woman just looked at her.

Rory cleared her throat and tried to make small talk, so she wouldn't leave on such a sour note with one of the people she was supposed to win over. "I've been on this road for quite a while and haven't seen any houses. Where is everyone?"

The woman was reluctant to answer, but her natural courtesy overcame her hostility. "We're a small tribe, but the houses are there. Most of them are set deep in the woods and aren't easily visible from the road. As for the people, many are employed off the reservation."

Rory started to thank her, but the woman cut her off. "Excuse me, I have work to do."

"Of course." Rory picked up her package and her can of soda. "You've been very kind."

The woman waited until Rory had left her store, then went to the door to watch her walk to the car.

With the package in one hand and the steering wheel in the other, Rory turned right out of the large driveway in front of the store and got back on the dirt road. She watched closely for landmarks the woman had mentioned.

It was a long, winding drive. This time, though, there was light traffic and she managed to spot some homes.

And then it got lonely. No more cars. No more houses. According to the map, she was nearing the hills.

Occasionally she would hit a straight stretch of road that enabled her to see the hills in the distance. They were higher than she'd expected because most of Wisconsin seemed to be so flat. And from where she was, they looked lush and green, thick with trees.

The road took her straight to the foot of the first hill where, in an area that had clearly already been stripped of foliage, she found the huge mining vehicles looming over her, their engines silent. Battered cars and trucks were strategically parked to prevent the mining vehicles from moving in any direction. Men and women sat on the hoods and trunks of the cars, cans of soda and beer in their hands. The dozen or so workmen who were there to operate the machinery were sitting on the ground in the shade, talking. It didn't matter to them if they couldn't work. They got paid anyway. Rory could almost hear the *ca-ching* of her uncle's dollars being thrown away.

Heads turned as she drove up in her shiny new rental car and parked near the men her uncle had hired. As she got out of the car, one of the men left his shady spot and walked over, his hand extended. "Joe McDermott, foreman. Are you the attorney?"

"Hi. Yes, I'm Rory Milbourne."

He looked her up and down suggestively. "You don't look like any attorney I've ever seen."

She pointedly declined his hand and met his rude gaze head-on. "Do you have a problem with the way I look?" she asked quietly so as not to be overheard.

He made no attempt to hold his growing smile in check. "No problem at all."

She leaned in closer to him, her eyes still on his. "Because if you do, I can arrange to have you taken off this job."

"I told you, I have no problem."

"I'm glad we understand each other. Tell me what's going on."

His smirk was replaced with a look of smoldering anger. Joe McDermott wasn't used to being spoken to that way. Not by men and certainly not by a woman. "Not a damn thing is happening, Ms. Milbourne." He spat out the "Ms." in such a way as to make it profane.

Rory ignored his tone. "Have you spoken with them?"

"We've said all we have to say. They won't move. That's why you're here."

"Thank you." Rory instantly put the foreman and his attitude out of her mind. Taking a deep breath and straightening her shoulders, she turned and headed for the protestors.

Even as she approached the other side, a motorcycle roared to a stop next to one of the pickups. A tall man with straight black hair that reached halfway down his back lowered the kickstand, climbed off and walked toward her. "Who are you?" he asked without any preliminaries.

"Rory Milbourne. I'm one of the attorneys for Milbourne Corporation. And you are?" she asked politely.

"Blackhawk."

For what seemed like an eternity, the two of them just stared at each other. She vaguely noticed that he wore a narrow leather thong around his neck and that a silver feather dangled from his right ear. But it was his intelligent dark eyes set in a magnificently carved face that held her attention.

Rory had to smile to herself. Held her attention? The man took her breath away.

When he spoke again, she actually jumped. "I'm sorry," she apologized. "What did you say?"

Daniel had been doing his own share of staring. Her eyes were a beautiful midnight blue with dark lashes and brows that contrasted with her shoulder-length golden reddish hair. Her skin was pale and smooth. Her lips were full and perfectly shaped. She wore the barest hint of lipstick.

"I asked what relation you are to William Milbourne."

"His niece."

She suddenly remembered her manners and held out her hand.

Daniel took it in his and held it. His eyes narrowed. *He knew this woman.*

Rory was taken aback by the intensity of his look. She retrieved her hand, still warm from his touch, and suddenly couldn't think of a thing to say.

"Why are you here?" asked Daniel.

His question snapped her back. "Because we have a problem."

"You mean that 'you' have a problem."

"I meant what I said. We have to settle this dispute."

"The only settlement is for you and your men to leave the reservation."

Rory tried to be reasonable. "I was hoping we could talk...."

"We've heard all the words, Ms. Milbourne. No matter how you arrange them, they all say the same thing."

"Maybe. Maybe not. What I'm looking for is a compromise that we can all live with."

Daniel looked at her for a long, silent moment. "You appear to be a fairly bright person," he said finally.

"Thank you," she said dryly.

"You tell me what kind of compromise is possible in a situation like this. Either you mine the land or you don't. There isn't a halfway point and there can be no compromise. What we want—what we demand—is that your men and your machinery leave our land."

Rory was usually slow to anger, but she could feel her temper rising. "We have a legal right to mine in these hills."

"And we have a moral right to keep our land from being destroyed."

"For heaven's sake, you're not even using this part of the reservation."

"What do you mean by 'using'?"

"There are no homes. No utilities. It's not as though people live here."

"That's right. We've kept it pure. The forest here is virgin. The land is the same as it was when we first came to inhabit it. These hills are sacred to us."

Rory inwardly rolled her eyes. Mumbo jumbo. But of course she couldn't say that.

Daniel looked at her for a long moment. "Why," he asked quietly, "when your people have taken so much from us over the years, can't you allow us even this small piece of land to call our own?"

His question made sense, but Rory was there to represent her uncle's interests, not Blackhawk's. "Mr. Blackhawk..."

"Doctor."

"Excuse me?"

"Dr. Blackhawk."

Rory couldn't hide her surprise. This man with hair halfway down his back, dressed in faded jeans and a blue chambray shirt, was a doctor? "Doctor of what?" she asked suspiciously.

"Medicine."

Oh. She got it. "So this is like a tribal thing?"

"It's more like a Harvard thing."

Her smile was more than a little tinged with embarrassment. "Oh. Sorry."

He didn't return the smile.

Rory cleared her throat and started again. This wasn't going well at all. She couldn't remember ever having been so clumsy. "Doctor, the reason I'm here is to calmly sit down with you, your grandfather and whoever else has decision-making power and offer you a fair return on the copper we remove."

"A fair return?"

"A percentage of our profits."

"You think this is about money?"

"I think nearly everything is about money in one form or another."

"You're very cynical for a woman so young," he said quietly.

"I'm probably not as young as you think. And what you consider cynicism is merely practicality. But to get back to the issue at hand, what I think is being lost in all of this is the fact that when the mining is finished, the land will be yours once again. You will have lost nothing and gained millions of dollars."

"The money won't replace what you destroy."

"We aren't here to destroy anything. All we want to do is remove the copper."

"And we're telling you that we don't want the copper removed."

Rory was at a loss. How was she supposed to reason with someone this stubborn? "In case you haven't reviewed the agreement we made with the government, it says that we promise to restore the land to its original condition when we're finished."

"Don't be naive, Ms. Milbourne. How can you restore the thousands of old trees that will have to be cut down? What about the displaced wildlife? The water will become polluted. The earth will have to be moved in order for you to access the copper."

"All right," she agreed. "Perhaps the words 'original condition' are a bit misleading. But I assure you that we'll leave behind inhabitable land. These are things we can talk about."

Daniel looked at her for a long moment. "No."

"Dr. Blackhawk," she said in exasperation, "you're not hearing me. We have a legal right to be here. We have a legal right to mine this land. If we wanted to, we could have all of you arrested this minute and taken away.''

''Do it.''

''That's not the way we want to go. We prefer to talk this out, like reasonable men and women.''

''We have no intention of 'talking this out,' as you say. We've told you no and we stand by that.''

The Native American men and women watching them had, one by one, been sliding off their cars and standing almost at attention as they watched the two of them.

'' 'We' meaning who?'' she asked.

''All of us.''

''But 'all' of you don't know about our offer of cutting the residents of the reservation in on a percentage of our profits.''

''It won't make a difference.''

''Then I assume you won't have a problem with me taking my offer directly to the people.''

''You can do what you wish in that regard.''

''We truly don't want to have to take you to court.''

''That, of course, is up to you.''

''Lawsuits are expensive to fight.''

He nodded.

''A thing like that could bankrupt your tribe.''

Daniel looked at her for a long moment. He knew a little more about the Milbourne Corporation than she thought. ''And your company.''

Rory didn't know what to do. The usual procedure in a standoff was to negotiate. What did you do when confronted with a man who refused to even discuss the possibility of a negotiation?

Daniel's dark eyes locked with hers. "I think I've made our position clear. As far as we're concerned, Ms. Milbourne, you, your men and your machinery are trespassing on our land. We're asking you to leave. And you should know that we will not be intimidated by any of your tactics."

Rory started to say something, but Daniel raised his hand to silence her. "This conversation is over."

Rory was furious. Turning on her heel, she strode to where the workers were sitting. Pointing to the obnoxious foreman she'd been such a hit with when she first arrived, she said, "Mr. McDermott, I'd like to have a word with you."

Daniel, now standing among his fellow protestors, followed her every movement with his eyes.

Rory and Joe walked to her car. "Did you hear what he said?" she asked.

"Yeah."

"I want a presence here twenty-four hours a day, even if you have to do it in shifts. There shouldn't be even a hint that we're backing down. If anything, I want our presence here to appear even stronger."

"Yes, ma'am."

"I also want you and your men to avoid any and all confrontations, either verbal or physical with these people. Be visible but keep to yourselves."

"Yes, ma'am." There was a subtle sarcasm behind his "ma'am" that Rory heard very clearly but chose to ignore.

She looked at the group across the invisible line—Daniel Blackhawk in particular. "What do you suppose he meant about not being intimidated by our tactics?"

"My guess is that it has something to do with a house that burned down last night. Rumor has it that they suspect our side of starting the fire."

"That's ridiculous."

He shrugged.

Rory studied the burly man in front of her. He had several days' growth of dark beard. His once-white T-shirt, stretched taut across his belly, was yellowed and stained. He had a way of looking at her that made Rory's skin crawl.

But...he was supposed to be the best at what he did, and she knew her uncle was paying him and his crew top dollar.

So the man leered. Lots of men leered. She could handle it.

She could handle him.

"All right. Just tell your men what I told you. I'll let you know what's going on as soon as I know."

"Sure."

She got into her car and sat there for a moment to organize her thoughts, unaware of Daniel's watchful gaze. Opening the console between the seats, she tapped her uncle's office number on the phone and put it to her ear. "Hi, Mary," she said when the secretary answered. "Is my uncle in?"

"Sure. I'll put you through."

As she waited, she looked through the windshield and straight into the enigmatic eyes of Daniel Blackhawk.

"Rory! What's happening?" Her uncle's gruff voice startled her, but she continued looking at Daniel.

"Nothing good, I'm afraid."

"Meaning?"

"I just finished speaking to Blackhawk. He refuses, in the absolute sense of the word, to negotiate."

"And the protestors?"

"Still out in force. They have the equipment blocked with their cars."

"This isn't good."

Rory had to smile. "I think that pretty much sums up the situation." She grew more serious. "Uncle Bill, I think what I have to do now, in addition to speaking directly to Gray Cloud, is take our case to the people on the reservation. I think once they know about the money, their response might be quite different."

"If that's what you think you should do, do it. But don't forget about Blackhawk and Gray Cloud. They wield a lot of power. You need to work some of your magic on them."

"I think the good doctor is all but immune to my particular brand of magic."

"Doctor?"

Rory sighed. "I'd explain, but frankly, it's not one of those moments I want to relive."

He had no idea what she was talking about. "Whatever. I don't need to remind you how much we need this deal."

"I know. You have my word that I'll do everything I can."

"That's my girl."

Now it was her turn to pause. "Uncle Bill, I don't quite know how to ask this."

"Fire away."

"Odd you should use that particular phrase. The foreman here said something about a fire on the reservation last night. Blackhawk seems to be under the impression that we had something to do with it."

"That's ridiculous."

"That's exactly what I said."

"We don't operate that way."

"I know." She paused. "You don't think that perhaps some loose cannon on the mining crew thought they were doing us a favor and..."

"No," he said firmly. "They're under Bruce's and my direct orders."

"I didn't think so, but I had to ask."

"If it comes up again, let Blackhawk know that if he says anything in public accusing me or anyone working for me of starting fires, I'll hit him with a slander suit so fast he'll wish he'd never been born."

"I'll pass the word."

"You take care of yourself."

"I will."

"Talk to Gray Cloud."

"Right."

"Call me as soon as you make some progress."

"It may take awhile."

"Not too long. Time is money."

"I know. Goodbye."

As she hung up the phone, she was still looking at Blackhawk. Even when he spoke to someone else, his eyes were on her.

He didn't frighten her exactly. Rory didn't know what she felt.

Something.

Starting the engine, she put the car into gear and forced herself to look away. With any luck, she wouldn't have to deal with him again. His grandfather was the one she'd approach.

She headed back in the same direction from which she'd come. She thought she'd be able to find her way, but the roads weren't marked and, one tree looked like the others to her.

Rory drove for several miles before coming to a fork. There was no sign. She had no idea which prong to take.

Swearing—just a little—under her breath, she looked for the bag the storekeeper had drawn the map on. She spotted it on the floor of the passenger side. She tried to reach it, but her seat belt prevented easy movement, so she popped it off.

Finally grasping the bag, she gave the directions a quick glance.

According to the map, she should go right. All right.

Still holding the bag, she started driving again. As she approached another possible turnoff, she checked the map again. When she looked back up, a deer ran out of nowhere right in front of her car. Rory jerked her steering wheel hard to the right to avoid hitting it, but she still felt a bump as though her left front fender had made contact. She tried to swerve the car back onto the road, but it was too late. It bounced into a ravine and came to rest against a tree with an impact that sent the now unbelted Rory into the windshield.

Chapter Three

Rory fell back into her seat, dazed, her heart hammering. She raised her fingers to her forehead and felt the warm stickiness of blood.

"Of all the stupid things to do," she said under her breath, and searched through her purse for some tissues to press against the wound. Rory *always* wore a seat belt. She'd worn one all the way from the airport to the reservation. Then in those few minutes when she had it off, this happened.

And the air bag hadn't worked.

And the deer had jumped in front of the car.

Oh, no. The deer.

Rory had to bang her shoulder against the car door

twice to get it open. She scrambled out of the ravine and onto the road to see if the deer was there.

It wasn't.

She was sure she'd hit it, though.

With the tissues getting increasingly blood soaked, she crossed the road and went into the woods where the deer must have run. She couldn't bear the thought of it suffering. What on earth she was going to do if she found it, Rory had no idea, but she wasn't thinking clearly. All she knew was that she had to do something.

As she walked, an unexpected wave of dizziness hit her. She grabbed the trunk of a tree and leaned against it for a minute until the feeling passed.

Then she started walking again, looking for the deer. She listened for any sound that might help her find it.

Her high heels sank into the carpet of dead pine needles with every step, making walking more difficult.

She really didn't feel well at all.

And there was no sign of the deer.

Rory sank to the ground, completely disregarding the damage to the golden white suit she was wearing, and leaned back against a tree. Blood continued to drip down her face. The soaked tissues were useless. She dropped them onto the ground and wiped the blood away with the back of her hand.

The forest was spinning around her.

She'd just sit for a few minutes, she thought, until the dizziness passed and then look for the deer again.

* * *

Daniel's motorcycle roared down the dirt road. He didn't normally travel this route home, but something compelled him to on this particular late afternoon.

He didn't see the car in the ditch until he was almost beside it. He skidded his bike to a quick stop, turned and came back. Even as he climbed down into the ravine, he realized that it was the car of the attorney he'd had the run-in with earlier.

And she wasn't in it.

He wasn't worried until he saw blood on the white paint of the driver's door which was open. Daniel leaned in and looked around. There was a purse, an unopened can of soda, a small paper bag with postcards inside and more blood.

He knew from having watched her earlier that she had a car phone. Opening the console, he pulled it out and punched in the number for the tribal police headquarters. "Get me Jake Troyat," he said abruptly when the operator answered.

A moment later Jake was on the phone. "What's up?"

"There's a car off the road about ten miles south of the general store. The driver is missing and, judging from the bloodstains, appears to be injured."

"Any identification?"

"Her name is Rory Milbourne." He paused. "Jake, she's William Milbourne's niece and attorney."

"And she's missing? Great. Can you tell what happened?"

"Only that she ran off the road."

Jake had to ask the question. "On her own or did she have a little help?"

"I don't know. Just get out here."

"I can be there in thirty minutes."

"Okay. I'm going to take a look and see what I can find. She's got to be around here somewhere. She didn't leave the hills all that long ago. The engine is still warm."

Daniel tossed the phone onto the seat and looked around. Following the trail of tire tracks, he was able to trace the path the car had taken from the road to the ravine, realizing what had happened. The hoofprints of a deer were just in front of the car's skid marks. She had apparently turned into the ditch in a successful effort to avoid hitting the animal, and hurt herself in the process.

So where had she gone?

He walked down the road until he was parallel with the car. There in the dirt were high heel marks. And they led across the road and into the woods.

He had already started following them when he heard the howl of a wolf in the distance.

Everything was so still. Rory had never heard such silence. She was used to hearing traffic and voices and sirens. She hadn't realized how comforting those sounds were until they were gone.

But gradually the silence was replaced with noises: odd noises. Noises she couldn't identify. Bug and creature noises that sent chills down her citified spine.

And eyes.

She was being watched. She could feel it. Rory turned her head to the right and found herself looking into a pair of unblinking golden eyes no more than ten feet away. The wolf was motionless.

Feeling as if she might have a heart attack from the shock, Rory inched her way up the tree into a standing position, her back tight against the trunk. She closed her eyes for a moment against the throbbing in her head. Maybe she was hallucinating, she thought optimistically.

No such luck. When she opened her eyes, the wolf was still there, still watching.

Rory swallowed hard. Her mind was racing, but she couldn't think of a single way out of this situation.

The wolf suddenly raised his nose to the sky and let out an ear-piercing howl.

Oh, God, thought Rory, he was calling his friends. She knew it. She was going to end her life as a doggy treat.

A hint of a breeze rustled in the trees and blew a curl across her face. Rory just left it there, terrified that any movement would provoke the wolf to attack.

It howled again.

Her heart sank further.

And then a man appeared out of nowhere beside the wolf. A man more relieved than he could say that he'd found her and she appeared to be all right.

Rory stared at him as he scratched the animal's head and said something to it in a language Rory didn't understand.

The wolf disappeared into the woods.

Rory barely noticed. Her gaze was riveted on the man—Blackhawk.

She felt quite distanced from herself as she watched him approach. Her vision was ever so slightly blurry, but she would have known him anywhere just by the way he moved.

Strange that she should know how he moved.

Daniel said nothing as he tilted her face toward the fading light. She stared at him without embarrassment, her eyes moving over his fiercely beautiful features.

Her gaze came to rest on his mouth, his incredible mouth.

"Ms. Milbourne, you're going to need about three stitches to close that gash," he said matter-of-factly, as he looked into her eyes to see if she'd understood.

Rory blinked twice in what appeared to be slow motion as she looked at him. "Stitches?"

"That's right."

"Is there a hospital nearby?"

"No, but there's a clinic. I'll take you."

She shook her head and winced. "No, thank you. Just get me out of the woods and I'll take myself."

"This is no time to be stubborn."

"I'm never stubborn. I'll have you know I'm one of the most reasonable people you'll ever meet. Just point me toward my car and I'll find my own way to the hospital. I'm fine." Even as she said the words, a wave of dizziness washed over her.

He caught her hand and put his strong arm around her waist. "Still fine?" he asked.

She gave him what nominally passed for a glare. Under the circumstances, it was the best she could do.

Without saying anything else, and most certainly without Rory's permission, Daniel lifted her in his arms.

She stared fuzzily at him, her face inches from his. "What are you doing?"

"Carrying you," he said as he started to walk.

"Well, stop it."

"You're in no condition to walk."

Rory had automatically put her arm around his neck. She now retrieved it and crossed both her arms across her breasts. "This is ridiculous."

And then it happened.

It started with a chill that went through her entire body, and then a surge of nausea rolled through her. "Put me down," she gasped as she struggled against him. "Please! Now!"

Daniel set Rory on her feet. She immediately dropped to her knees, her hands flat on the ground in front of her and her head bent as spasms racked her body. He knelt beside her, holding her hair away from her face and stroking her back with a gentle hand.

Rory hadn't eaten since early morning, but the fact that nothing came up didn't make the spasms any less miserable. And they kept coming, one after another. Just when she thought it was all over, another one hit her.

Still on her knees, Rory leaned into Daniel for support. She was embarrassed and exhausted. "I'm sorry."

"We'll rest here until you feel better."

She nodded weakly into his shoulder and closed her eyes. "I just need a minute."

His arm went around her, steadying her.

The thought crossed her mind that she was in the woods on a reservation, completely at the mercy of a long-haired man who considered her his enemy—and she couldn't remember ever feeling safer.

After a few minutes, she reluctantly pushed herself away from him. "I'm feeling a little better."

Once again he lifted her effortlessly into his arms and started walking. This time Rory put her arm around his neck and rested her head on his shoulder. She was utterly, completely drained. "Thank you," she said softly, her mouth close to his ear.

The muscle in his jaw tightened.

"How did you find me?" she asked, without lifting her head.

"I saw your car and tracked you into the woods." His tone didn't encourage conversation.

"My car!" Rory raised her head and looked at him with eyes full of distress. "I think I hit a deer."

"No, you didn't," he said.

"Yes, I did."

He shifted her weight slightly. "The deer is fine."

"How do you know?"

"There's no disturbance of the deer's tracks at the point where the impact would have happened."

"You're sure?"

"Yes."

Rory put her head back on his shoulder. "That's good. I was worried."

"Is that why you went into the forest?"

She nodded and winced.

As they left the woods, he carried her up a ravine to the road where his motorcycle sat waiting. Jake, in uniform, was there checking out the car. He turned as they approached and climbed up the embankment. "I see you found her. What happened?"

"A deer ran in front of her car."

"You're sure it was a deer?"

"Yes."

"Thank heaven for that. Is she okay?"

"Yes, she is," answered Rory, growing tired of being left out of the conversation.

"No," corrected Daniel. "She has a nasty cut on her forehead that needs a few stitches."

"Three," she offered.

"And she might have a little concussion."

"I see," said Jake. "Is there anyone you'd like notified about the accident Ms. Milbourne?"

"No, thank you." There was no sense in worrying her uncle.

"Are you staying in this area with someone?"

"No. I'm going to stay at a motel."

"That's out," said Daniel. "At least for tonight. You clearly need to be looked after."

"So what are you going to do with her?" asked Jake.

"Keep her with me," he said unenthusiastically. "If all goes well I'll take her to the motel tomorrow."

Jake looked closely at his friend. "Are you sure you want to do that? I could arrange for someone else…"

"Thanks, Jake. I'll take care of her."

"All right. I'll get her things and drop them off at your place and then arrange a tow for the car."

"Thank you," said Rory.

Jake flashed her a smile. He didn't care if she was Milbourne's niece. He liked her. Slapping Daniel on the shoulder, he went back into the ravine.

Daniel carried Rory to his motorcycle.

She looked down at it from the safety of his arms. "And what exactly is this?"

"My motorcycle."

"Oh, no," she said, shaking her head. "There's no way I'm getting on that thing."

"You don't have a choice."

"Put me down right now."

Daniel obliged her by setting her on the machine and climbing on behind her.

"This isn't what I meant and you know it." She started to get off, but he held her in place.

"Look, Ms. Milbourne, don't make this any more difficult than it already is. Your car is wrecked. Jake came on his motorcycle and I came on mine. This is the only way I have of getting you to the clinic and this is the way you're going. Now I strongly suggest you cooperate."

"Or what?"

"I'll strap you to the gas tank."

"That's not funny."

"It wasn't intended to be." He pulled her back against his chest. "Now sit still and shut up."

Daniel released the kickstand and started the engine with a powerful downward thrust of his right leg.

Rory's body was completely stiff in its resistance to the man behind her.

"Relax," he told her. "I'm not going to hurt you."

There was the slightest of hesitations before she did as he asked and let her body settle against his.

The muscle in his jaw moved again. As the bike surged forward, he balanced both of them and raised his feet off the ground. Rory could feel his strong thighs against the backs of her legs, holding her safely and steadily in place.

She didn't like this at all.

As the bike picked up speed, she was pushed against his chest even more. His arms formed a barrier on either side of her so she couldn't have fallen off if she'd wanted to.

After a five-minute ride, he parked the bike in front of a tiny building with a hand-lettered sign over the front door that read Clinic. Once again Daniel scooped her into his arms and carried her inside.

They went through a small, empty waiting room into an examining room. He set her on a metal table, then went to the wall switch and flicked on the lights.

Rory watched Daniel as he went to the sink and washed his hands, then came back to her, turning on a light with a movable arm and shining it in her face.

She pushed his hand away. "Stop that. It hurts."

"Don't be such a baby."

She squinted and tried to turn away from the light, but Daniel held her chin with a firm gentleness between his thumb and forefinger as he examined her forehead. "You definitely need stitches," he said after a moment.

"Will I have a scar?"

"Yes, but not a very noticeable one. The gash is near your hairline. Hold your hair away from your face."

Rory raised her hands and pulled her hair into a ponytail.

Daniel cleaned the cut and anesthetized the skin around it as best he could. It was still going to hurt.

Rory wouldn't give him the satisfaction of flinching again. Baby, indeed.

When he took his first stitch, Daniel fully expected her to lash out at him, but she didn't even move. When he took the second stitch and she didn't move, he looked at her face. He'd never seen a more determined expression. He thought it was kind of cute.

"I'm sorry if this hurts."

Rory didn't say anything.

He finished the last stitch. "All done," he said. He went back to the sink and rinsed a cloth with warm soapy water then walked back to Rory. She looked up at him as he ran it gently over her face and hands to clean off the blood and dirt.

As his eyes met hers, Daniel's hand paused in midstroke.

"What?" asked Rory, suddenly alert when she saw his strange look. "Is it more serious than you thought?"

"Excuse me?" It took him a moment to get his conversational bearings.

"My injury. Is it worse than you thought?"

"Oh, no," he said as he finished cleaning her up. "No. Nothing like that."

"So I'm all right?"

"You will be."

Rory let her hair fall as she watched him. "Since we're both here, can we talk about the copper mining?"

Daniel cut her off. "No. I said everything I had to say this afternoon. As far as I'm concerned, that's the end of it. You can go home tomorrow and tell your uncle to dig in someone else's sandbox."

"And you think I'm stubborn." Rory slid off the table to her feet. "You haven't heard the last of..." Her voice drifted off as the room spun around her.

Daniel crossed the room in two strides to catch her before she hit the ground.

"This is humiliating," she said weakly.

For the first time since they'd met, Daniel almost smiled. "You're not used to depending on anyone else, are you?"

"Not really."

"Well, for tonight at least you don't have any choice. You're weak, dizzy and you probably have one hell of a headache."

"I do," she admitted.

"Then let me take care of you. I'm a doctor. It's what I'm supposed to do. Stop fighting me."

She leaned against him. "I'm really tired," she said.

"I know."

"I want to go home."

"Tonight you're going home with me."

"Okay."

Once again Daniel lifted her in his arms and carried her to his motorcycle.

Rory didn't fight it. She was smart enough to know that she needed the help he offered.

As the sun had begun to set, it had grown progressively cooler. Rory shivered involuntarily. Daniel, who seemed to notice everything, placed her on the cycle, sat behind her and settled her body against his in such a way that his body kept her warm. He released the kickstand and started the big engine.

The machine roared to life. It was interesting. If her head hadn't hurt so badly she would have enjoyed the ride and the way the bike seemed to vibrate its way right through her. Given the right circumstances, she thought, it could have been very sexy.

As it was, she thought her head was going to explode.

She closed her eyes against the wind as they rode and didn't open them until Daniel stopped in front of a log cabin on the lake. Rory couldn't see it very well, because the sun was just setting in a flaming orange ball on the lake's horizon.

She tightly shut her eyes again. Light was not her friend. At least not at the moment.

Daniel snapped the kickstand into place and lifted Rory in his arms. He pushed open his unlocked door with his foot and carried her across a wide expanse of open floor to a bed. As he lay her down, even though he was gentle, Rory had the disquieting feeling that he couldn't unload her fast enough.

Her eyes followed him as he struck a match and held it to the wick of an old-fashioned lantern. At first the flame flickered and danced, but then it grew steady and strong, chasing the darkness from the center of the cabin but leaving the corners in shadow. This kind of light she could live with, she thought.

Daniel took a jar from a kitchen shelf and carried it to Rory. Sitting on the edge of the bed, he raised the bandage and, with a light touch, dotted some paste from the jar onto her cut.

Rory wrinkled her nose at the strong smell. It wasn't particularly unpleasant, just different. "What's that?"

"Indian herbal medicine. It'll prevent infection and help the wound to heal."

She didn't trust anything that didn't come with a label. "Are you sure?"

He seemed to be going out of his way not to look at her. "My people have been using it for centuries." He said it nicely enough, but there was a hint of admonishment in his voice.

"You do that a lot."

"Do what?"

"Distinguish between your people and others."

"What's your point?"

"Why do you do that?"

"Because distinctions exist." He replaced her bandage.

"So you like being segregated from the rest of the American population?"

"In some ways, yes. We have our own traditions and beliefs and don't want them any more diluted than they've already become."

"But that's what America's all about. We're all blended from different cultures."

"Your America. Not mine."

"There you go again."

Daniel set the small jar of salve on the table beside the bed. "Do you honestly think Native Americans are the only people in search of their roots?"

"No, of course not. But you're the only people doing it in this kind of isolation from the rest of the country."

"I can see why you're confused," he said as he went to a closet. "It's quite a country you've made for yourselves. You go to the trouble of stealing it from us, you turn it into a land where neither women nor men are safe walking down a street in broad daylight, and now you generously want us to be a part of it. Thanks but no thanks." He took one of his shirts off a hanger and tossed it onto the bed. "Put that on. You can use it to sleep in."

Rory absently picked up the shirt and held it. "Is life really so much better here?"

He turned to look at her. "We may be poor, but you can walk our roads in the middle of the night in complete safety. We have a code of honor that is still intact, and we take care of our own and those entrusted to us. Without the reservation, we'd all be scattered to the four winds, along with our traditions, our religion, our way of life—even our language. What you have to understand is that this land—this reservation—is our country. It's all we have left. When you come here with your people and your trucks to dig into our earth and take what's there, it's tantamount to an invasion.''

She thought that was putting it a little too strongly, but she didn't have the energy to argue.

As Daniel walked back to the kitchen counter, Rory self-consciously slipped her arms out of her suit jacket and held it protectively in front of her as she took off her bra and put on his shirt.

Sliding off the bed, she steadied herself with one hand on the mattress while she stepped out of her skirt, folded the ruined clothes neatly and put them on the floor beside the bed.

"How's your stomach feeling?'' asked Daniel.

"Better,'' she said. She settled under the warmth of the quilt and leaned back against the pillows.

He brought her a mug of broth. "Drink it,'' he said. He took her hands and cupped them around the mug. "It'll help dispel the weakness without making you feel ill.''

Their eyes met and held.

Every time the man touched her, it was like an electrical shock. "Thank you.''

He let go of her hands and walked away.

The wolf who'd eyed her in the forest came in through the open door and settled on a rug in front of the unlit fireplace. He stared at Rory with unblinking yellow eyes.

Rory nearly choked on her broth. "Um, excuse me," she said, as calmly as she could manage.

Daniel was standing in the open kitchen area with his back toward her.

When he didn't respond, she said it louder. "Excuse me!"

He turned his head. "What?"

"I just thought you might want to know that you have a wolf in your house."

Daniel looked disinterestedly at the wolf and turned back to what he was doing. "I know."

"You know?" she asked in disbelief. "That's it? You aren't going to do anything about it?"

"That's right. He comes and goes as he pleases."

"So he belongs to you?"

"He belongs to no one."

"Aren't you afraid of him?"

"Of course not."

"So what you're saying is that I don't have anything to worry about here."

"He's apparently appointed himself your protector. He's the one who found you in the woods first."

Rory wasn't entirely convinced. She sat a little straighter as she drank her broth, her eyes unwaveringly on the wolf.

Daniel started to walk toward the door.

"You're not leaving me, are you?" Her voice was more panicked than she intended.

A hint of a smile touched his mouth for the first time since they'd met. "It's a little chilly. I'm going to get some wood from the porch to build a fire."

As he left, she kept her eyes on the wolf. He stretched out, his head on his paws, eyes open, watching her.

Rory allowed herself to relax a little. That was definitely not an attack posture.

Daniel returned with an armload of wood. She watched while he laid the fire and lit it. It caught almost instantly and made the cabin seem wonderfully cozy.

"Are you finished drinking the broth?" he asked, and walked toward her.

"Yes, thank you. I didn't think I was hungry, but I was."

He took the mug from her hands and set it on the table beside her. "How's your head feel?"

"It hurts."

"It probably will for a few days."

"It serves me right for not having on my seat belt. I still can't believe I did that."

He leaned over, took one of the pillows out from under Rory's head and settled her against the remaining ones. Then he pulled the quilt up around her.

Rory smiled.

"What?" he asked as he leaned over her.

"This is nice. I can't remember the last time I was tucked in by someone."

His face was close to hers. He said nothing. She said nothing. Her smile faded. Rory had never in her life been as aware of the essence of a man as she was at that moment. She could feel her heart beating. Loudly. Surely he could hear it, she thought.

Daniel straightened away from her. He did hear a heart beating, but it was his own. "I'll have to wake you every couple of hours because of the nature of your injury," he said efficiently.

It was as though being near him had robbed her of her voice. She nodded.

Her eyes followed him across the room as he moved the lantern. She cleared her throat and willed her heart to slow down. "Don't you have electricity?"

It took Daniel a moment to answer. "I usually use solar energy. I just happen to like lantern light for my home. It's less intrusive." He turned to look at her. "Good night."

"I'm sorry to be so much trouble."

Daniel sat in a leather chair near the fireplace, his feet propped up on a footstool. "It's not your fault," he said. He set the lantern on the table beside him and picked up a book. "Try to get some sleep."

Rory watched him from the safety of the shadows. He didn't appear to be a man who smiled a lot, despite the grooves in his cheeks. By the same token, he also struck her as a man slow to anger. Her gaze moved over his long hair. She'd never liked men in long hair. And yet she couldn't imagine him with anything else.

Daniel raised his hand to turn a page.

He had long fingers. She could imagine him as a surgeon. She could imagine lots of things, but she tried to stick with the medical angle. What on earth was he, a Harvard-educated doctor, doing here?

Daniel Blackhawk was one intriguing mystery after another.

Her eyes grew heavy. It was too much effort to keep them open. Besides, her head felt better when they were closed.

She sighed aloud without realizing it. She couldn't remember the last time she'd felt so completely safe and content.

Or maybe she could, she thought drowsily. There was that time when she was ten. . . .

Daniel set his book aside and leaned his head against the back of his chair. The more he tried not to think about the woman in his bed, the more he thought about her.

He got up from his chair and walked outside to the porch. Distance, he thought, even a few feet, would help.

But it didn't.

He stayed outside for nearly an hour in unmoving silence, staring at the lake.

And then Daniel went back. As he sat on the edge of the bed, it sank under his weight. He watched her for a long time before reaching out with a gentle hand and pushing her hair away from her face. "Wake up," he said softly, and he stroked her skin with his thumb, skin that was every bit as soft and smooth as it looked.

Rory's eyelids fluttered but she didn't wake.

"Come on," he said a little louder. "Talk to me."

Rory was in a lovely, woozy place and she didn't want to leave.

Daniel took one of her hands in his and briskly rubbed it. "Open your eyes, Rory."

She frowned, wishing he'd just be quiet and let her sleep. It was with great reluctance that she finally did as he asked. At first the face above hers was a blur, but Daniel gradually came into focus. Her reluctance vanished.

"Do you know where you are?" he asked.

Her mouth curved into a smile that transformed her already lovely face as she gazed into his eyes. "With you." There was a world of happiness in the way she said those two words.

Daniel refused to allow himself to be affected by her. "Be more specific."

"With you, *darling*."

The grooves in his cheeks deepened. He couldn't help it. All of her lawyerly dignity went right out the window. "You're going to kick yourself in the morning if you remember any of this."

"Any of what?"

He ignored her question. "Pay attention. Besides being with me, where are you?"

"Whispering Pines Reservation."

"Very good. Do you remember how you got here?"

"I wrecked my car and hit my head."

"Good girl. Go back to sleep."

"I couldn't possibly."

She was out like a light before the last word was uttered.

With a hint of a smile still evident, Daniel shook his head and pulled the quilt up around her again.

He stayed there for a long time, looking at her, wondering how it was that she was so utterly familiar to him. He looked at her lips and felt as though he knew what it would feel like to kiss her—as though he'd done it before.

And yet he knew he'd never seen her.

Jake knocked on the door and opened it, as he was accustomed to doing. "I brought her purse and suitcase," he said in a whisper when he spotted Rory asleep. "Where do you want them?"

Daniel rose from the bed. He pointed toward a chair near the bathroom door. "There will be fine."

After he set down the luggage, Jake stood over the bed and looked at her. "How's she doing?"

"She'll be all right."

"Her car is a mess. The rental agency is having it towed. She'll have to call them herself if she wants another one."

"She won't be needing one. I'm sure I can find someone who can take her to the airport tomorrow."

"I don't know, friend. She didn't sound to me as though she were planning to leave."

"There's nothing here for her."

"I don't know, Daniel," said Jake with a shake of his head. "She doesn't look like a quitter."

Daniel went to his chair by the fire and sat down. "Maybe not. I just know that I want her gone."

"I thought you liked pretty women."

"Everyone likes pretty women."

"Ah. So it's this particular one you want to get rid of."

Daniel, his eyes on Rory, said nothing.

Jake watched his friend curiously. He knew Daniel well enough to know when he was troubled. "What's wrong?"

Daniel shook his head. "I can't explain it. There's just something about her...." He let the sentence hang.

Jake didn't know what to say to his friend. Instead of using words, he gripped Daniel's shoulder and quietly left.

Daniel leaned back in his chair, his head against the cushion, and gazed at Rory.

The night crawled by as he sat there. Minutes ticked into hours. And as the hours passed, an inescapable awareness started to grow deep inside him.

Suddenly his heart slammed against his ribs and he sat up straight.

It was her.

But it couldn't be. She was white.

He went to the bed and stood staring down at her. With a gentle hand, he pushed her tousled curls away from her face. Rory opened her midnight blue eyes and looked straight at Daniel. More asleep than not, she took his hand in hers and held it against her cheek. The tiniest of smiles touched her lips as she closed her eyes and went back to sleep.

Daniel didn't try to take his hand away, simply left it in hers as he sat on the edge of the bed.

There was a nearly unbearable tightness in his chest that grew and spread. His grandfather had been right. He recognized her.

And even as he gazed upon the face of the woman he'd carried in his heart for twenty-five years, there was a terrible reality with which he had to deal.

His love was also his enemy.

How had this happened?

Chapter Four

Rory raised her hand to her head and touched the bandage that covered her wound. She opened her eyes, then quickly closed them. It was too bright. Way too bright.

She blinked a few times until she was finally able to open her eyes without squinting. Much.

Sunlight insisted on streaming through the windows. Where was gloom when you needed it?

As she gradually focused on the rough-hewn beamed ceiling, it took her a moment to register what she was seeing. Beamed ceiling? Where on earth was she?

Raising herself up on her elbows, Rory looked around the one-room cabin. It was open and spacious. The walls were made from logs except for the stone wall that held the fireplace. The windows were long and wide, bringing a lot of the outdoors inside. And the furniture—it was masculine and comfortably worn. She saw her suitcase and purse on a chair not far from the bed.

And then it came back to her. At least she thought it came back to her. Long hair. Strong arms. Dark eyes.

Daniel Blackhawk.

Rory gingerly sat up the rest of the way and looked around more thoroughly. There was certainly no man there now.

She swung her bare legs over and put her feet on the ground. So far, so good, she thought.

Then she stood up and waited to see what would happen.

Her head hurt, but compared to the way it had throbbed yesterday, this was nothing.

Perspective was definitely a good thing, she thought.

Rory padded to her purse, pulled out her dark sunglasses and put them on. She looked around the suddenly darkened cabin and smiled. This was much better.

Then she crossed the wood floor to the open door and stepped onto the porch.

It was a beautiful, beautiful morning. Even with the dark glasses, she shielded her eyes from the sun with her hand as she looked around. The sky was a cloudless blue. The air was scented with pine and earth and early morning dew. She'd never smelled anything like it.

As she was looking around, Rory saw a movement out of the corner of her eye. She turned her head just in time to see Daniel Blackhawk walk out of the lake as naked as the day he was born, water streaming down his bronzed body. Rory gasped in surprise and took a backward step into the safety of the cabin.

Then she thought about it for a moment.

Pulling her sunglasses down her nose so she could see over the top of the frames, she leaned forward just enough to poke her head outside. Daniel was still naked, drying himself with a towel.

Oh, dear.

Her eyes started their journey with his long, strong legs and worked their way up over his flat, muscled stomach, sculpted chest and shoulders. And that long, black hair.

Even as Rory was thinking that she couldn't believe she was doing this, she let her eyes travel back down his body.

The man was perfect.

He moved his head as though he were going to look up. Rory jerked her head back inside. Her eyes crossed with the sudden shot of pain, but there was no time to lose. As quickly as she could, she went back to the bed. And in the nick of time. Daniel walked in just as she sank onto the mattress. He was wearing jeans and no shirt.

Rory quickly pushed her glasses back up the bridge of her nose.

"Good," he said, walking toward the bed, "you're awake."

She couldn't think of a thing to say.

He took off her glasses and tossed them onto the bed, then took her chin between his thumb and forefinger and turned her toward the light as he examined her forehead. "You look much better this morning."

Her eyes were on his.

"You're a little flushed though." He touched the uninjured part of her forehead with the back of his hand. "You don't have a fever."

She lowered her eyes. "I'm fine. Really."

"Perhaps you had too much early morning fresh air."

Oh, no, she thought. He must have seen her watching him. Flushed cheeks? Another minute and she'd burst into flame.

"The stitches should come out in a few days," said Daniel as he walked away from her. "You can have your doctor do that for you when you get back to Chicago."

"When I get back to Chicago? I thought you said they could come out in a few days."

"That's right."

"Unless the matter of the copper mining is magically settled, I'll still be here."

Daniel turned around and looked at her. "What?"

Rory got to her feet. "Look, I appreciate everything you've done for me. I truly do. I don't know what would have happened to me if you hadn't found me yesterday. But the fact that I'm grateful to you as a person doesn't change the fact that I'm here as a lawyer. I came here for a reason, and I still have work to do."

Daniel looked at her for a long time without saying anything, then he turned away. "If that's the way you want it, get yourself cleaned up. I'll take you to the motel."

"Thank you."

"Jake came by last night. He said you'll need to rent a new car. The other one's been towed."

"All right."

"You know," he said quietly, and turned back to her, "your staying here isn't going to change anything. We aren't going to suddenly smack our foreheads and exclaim in wonder at our stupidity in not seeing just how right you were all along."

"You can never tell."

Daniel and Rory's gazes were locked in an impossible-to-break standoff until Daniel spoke.

"You'll find the bath through the door near the bed. Your suitcase is on the chair."

"Thank you."

Rory, her heart hammering uncontrollably, turned, walked to her suitcase, took out what she needed and went into the bathroom. With her back pressed against the door, she stood without moving for several seconds.

Control, she thought. That was the key. She prided herself on her control and discipline. That was what had gotten her so far at such an early age.

And yet it seemed as though Daniel somehow stripped her of that control every time she was with him.

Well, at least she was aware of it. That was half the battle as far as she was concerned.

Setting her things down, she leaned over the sink and looked critically at herself in the mirror. She wasn't a pretty sight. No makeup. Smudges of blood on her face and caked in her hair. She was beyond a mess.

Leaning closer, she lifted the bandage and looked at her forehead. She had to admit that it wasn't as bad as she'd expected, though the stitches were rather ugly. The dark bruise surrounding it looked worse than the cut itself.

Daniel knocked.

Rory went on instant alert. "Yes?"

"Don't get your stitches wet."

She was surprised by his concern. "I won't."

She heard his footsteps walking away and turned her attention to the bathtub. It was an old-fashioned one with feet but there was definitely plumbing. The taps were old-fashioned, as well, but they worked. She turned the hot and the cold knobs and adjusted them until the temperature was just right.

Taking off Daniel's shirt, she hung it on the back of the door, then lowered herself into the tub, slowly sinking into the warm water until it came up to her neck.

She couldn't help a heartfelt "oooh" from escaping her lips. It felt wonderful.

Sinking further into the water, she wet her hair but not her face. She picked up her shampoo from the flat rim of the tub, squeezed some into the palm of her hand and then worked it into her hair. Then, while her hair was still lathered, she soaped her body and washed her face.

Clean had never felt so good.

Daniel knocked on the door again. "I'd appreciate it if you'd hurry up. I have to get to the clinic."

If she'd had her druthers, Rory would have spent the morning in the bath. But . . . she reluctantly sat up and unplugged the drain. As the water flowed out of the tub, she turned on the faucet and rather awkwardly maneuvered herself so that she was on her back to rinse out her hair without getting her forehead wet.

She stepped onto a towel she'd tossed onto the wood floor and carefully towel-dried her hair, then dressed in the coffee-colored trousers and creamy silk blouse she'd brought into the bathroom with her. This time when she looked in the mirror, she still wasn't thrilled with what she saw, but it was certainly better than it had been.

She looked through the drawers for a hair dryer but didn't find one. She should have known. Daniel Blackhawk was definitely not a hair dryer kind of guy.

As she got ready to leave, she felt as though she were going into battle. Pulling back her shoulders and tilting her chin, she opened the door and stepped into the line of fire.

No one was there.

What a disappointing letdown. All of that gearing up and the enemy was nowhere in sight. Rory didn't know whether to be relieved or disappointed.

She crossed the open floor of the cabin and stepped outside onto the porch. "Hello, there," called a cheery voice.

Rory turned to find a Native American woman about her own age sitting in one of the wood-slatted chairs. "Hello," said Rory as she walked toward her.

The other woman held out her hand. "I'm Susan Troyat." She shook Rory's hand and gestured toward the chair across from her. "Please, have a seat."

Rory was glad to have her back to the sun as she sat down. "Your name sounds familiar."

"My husband is Jake Troyat. He's with the tribal police." She smiled. "Actually, he is the tribal police."

"Oh," said Rory, nodding. "I met him yesterday. And I understand he brought my things from the car."

"That's right."

"If I don't see him, please thank him for me."

"Of course."

Rory turned in her seat slightly and, squinting her eyes against the sun, looked around. "Where's Daniel?"

"He asked me to tell you that he was called away to see a patient. He said he'd be back soon."

"Oh." Another letdown.

"How are the two of you getting along?"

Rory couldn't help the smile that touched her lips. "He says tomato, I say 'tomahto'."

Susan laughed. She was a lovely woman with chin-length dark hair and friendly, sparkling eyes. "I had a feeling things might be a little awkward."

"That's a kind way of putting it."

"When you get to know Daniel better, you'll discover that he's really a fine man. He feels very strongly, as do many of us, that we need to preserve what we have left, not tear it down."

"I know." Rory studied her face for a moment. "You sound as though you're one of the preservationists."

"I didn't used to be that way," she said. "But as I've grown older and given birth to a child of my own, it's become more and more important to me that those things that made my people who we are remain intact for my children, and my children's children, to learn from in their own lifetimes."

"But aren't you concerned that this obsession with the past will hold them back in life?"

"How?"

"By not enabling them to move forward with the rest of the country and join the mainstream."

Susan shook her head. "I've seen the mainstream and I don't think that's where I want my children to end up."

"I have to admit that's kind of hard to argue with."

Susan nodded. "What you have to understand is that I want the best of both worlds for my children, and I don't think they need to exclude one in order to succeed in the other."

"I see."

"I don't think you do. Not yet, anyway. It would be nice if you could spend some time here among us." She smiled. "Perhaps we could change your mind."

Rory leaned back in her chair. "I don't think your Dr. Blackhawk wants me to hang around."

"But you're going to anyway, aren't you?"

"Yes."

She nodded. "Jake described you to me last night. He said he didn't think you'd leave here until things were settled. Where are you going to stay?"

"I understand there's a motel nearby. I'll rent a room there. Daniel might not like it, but that can't be helped."

"Good for you. Daniel gets his way far too often. Most women take one look at him and their wills buckle—not to mention their knees."

"If you like that type," said Rory, trying her very best to sound dismissive.

"And so many women don't," said Susan dryly. "Tall, dark, gorgeous, reserved, well-educated."

Rory had to smile. "All right. I'll concede that he's an attractive man."

"You better believe he is. There isn't a woman in her right mind who wouldn't give her eyeteeth to have a man like Daniel Blackhawk fall in love with her."

"I think I'll keep my teeth."

Now it was Susan's turn to smile.

"I'm surprised he isn't married and procreating madly to carry on the family legacy," said Rory.

"I guess he hasn't met the right woman."

"If there is such a woman."

"There is. His grandfather told him."

"What?"

"Gray Cloud had a vision. He told Daniel that his woman would come to him, but so far she hasn't."

"A vision?" Rory asked skeptically.

Susan laughed good-naturedly. "Don't be too quick to judge. Visions are an important part of our lives."

"What exactly are they? Some kind of mystical thing?"

"It's a spiritual experience. We don't all have them. Usually it's just the wisest and holiest among us."

"And that would be Gray Cloud."

"Yes."

"And he had a vision about Daniel's future wife."

"That's right." Susan tilted her head as she studied Rory. "Who knows? Perhaps you're her."

Rory's smile grew. "Oh, I think it's pretty clear that Daniel Blackhawk and I are definitely not a vision kind of couple."

"You can never tell about these things."

"Apparently some of you can."

Susan laughed again. "I like you. Jake told me I would."

"Even though we're on opposing sides?"

She shrugged. "What's friendship without a little challenge? It's the struggle that makes us strong."

Rory leaned forward, her elbows on her knees. "Susan, may I ask you for a favor?"

"Of course."

"Would you introduce me to Gray Cloud?"

Susan pushed her short hair away from her face. For the first time in the conversation, she hesitated. "I can't."

"Why?"

"It's not my place. He's Daniel's grandfather and Daniel should be the one to introduce you."

"I don't think he will."

"Ask. He might surprise you."

Rory would rather have had Susan do it, but she nodded. "Okay." She leaned back in her chair, turned her head and gazed into the woods. "There's something I'm curious about."

"What?"

"Why did Daniel come back here after he got his education? He could have gone anywhere."

"Because he's an honorable man. He gave his word to his grandfather."

"Do you think he wants to be here?"

Susan grew thoughtful. "When I was little, Daniel was like my big brother. I tagged after him everywhere. He never minded. My memory of Daniel as a child is that he was very serious, as he is as a man. He took his responsibilities to his family and his tribe to heart. And when he gave his word to someone, he kept it. Now I think he has one foot in our world and one foot in yours. I believe he is the kind of man who could fit into either culture with ease. But this reservation is where his heart is. The people who live here are where his responsibilities lie."

"I see."

"You'd like Daniel if you gave yourself a chance."

Rory smiled. "I don't need to like Daniel. I just need to be able to reason with him."

"That's something entirely different."

"So I'm finding out."

"I'll tell you right now, though, if you're hoping to get Daniel to change his mind about the mining, it's not going to happen."

"It has to happen," she said quietly. "And I don't have any choice but to make it."

Susan looked at her curiously. "Why is it so important?"

"Because I, too, gave my word. My uncle is counting on me and I'm not going to let him down."

Even as she finished saying the words, Rory heard the sound of Daniel's motorcycle approaching in the distance. Her senses went on instant alert.

Susan watched her new friend's expression with great interest as Daniel roared to a stop in front of the cabin, climbed off the cycle and walked toward them.

Susan greeted him with a smile.

Daniel leaned over and kissed her on the cheek. "What are you doing here?"

"That's a fine hello."

"Hello. What are you doing here?"

"Jake told me you had a houseguest. I just came by to meet her for myself."

"Now you've met her, so say goodbye. I'm taking her to the motel." He looked at Rory. "Are you ready to go?"

"Yes."

"I'll get the truck and take you." He walked around to the back of the cabin. A moment later she heard the sound of an engine starting and watched as Daniel drove around the cabin and stopped behind the motorcycle. Without saying anything, he went inside for her luggage, tossed it into the back of his truck, then stood by the open passenger door and waited for her to climb in.

Rory turned to Susan. "Is it just my imagination or does he seem to be in a hurry to get rid of me?"

"I don't think it's your imagination." Susan leaned forward and kissed Rory's cheek. "Take care of yourself. Call me if you need anything. You can get my number through information."

"I will. Thanks." She walked down the steps and had to brush by Daniel. Her heart jumped at the contact and her eyes went straight to his. Their expression was unreadable.

Was she the only one who felt the electricity between them? Couldn't he feel it, too?

She climbed into the truck and Daniel firmly closed the door after her, walked around the front of the truck, climbed into the driver's side and put it into gear.

It was an old vehicle—vintage, really. But it had been well taken care of over the years. While the outside was a little dusty, the inside was spotless.

They drove in silence down the winding dirt road. Since she didn't have to do the driving, it gave her a chance to look around. This time she was able to spot the narrow roads that disappeared into the woods and led to the homes. Every once in a while she'd spot a satellite dish looming out of seemingly nowhere. There was a tiny log cabin museum not far from the general store where she'd stopped the day before.

"Why are all of the buildings I've seen made from logs?"

"Because it's an inexpensive natural resource for us. Of course we have homes made from clapboard, as well, and some brick, but the logs serve as better insulators against the rough winters."

That made sense.

"You might not be aware of this, but it was the Indians who taught the settlers how to build log cabins."

Rory looked at him in surprise. "I had no idea."

"We're a Woodland tribe. We tended to stay in one place, unlike the Plains Indians, who moved frequently and needed more mobile structures."

"Why did they move around?"

"To follow their food source."

"Buffalo?"

"Exactly."

"And you didn't have to follow your food?"

"Deer and antelope were our main source of food and clothing, but while we had to hunt them in the woods, as some of us still occasionally do today, they were usually plentiful and tended to stay in the same general area."

Silence once again fell between them as they drove. It took more than an hour to get from Daniel's house to the highway. Fifteen minutes later, Daniel pulled into the parking lot of a nondescript-looking motel that had a half-lit neon sign blinking the word *Vacancy*.

They both climbed out of the truck, walked around to the back and reached for her suitcase at the same time. As their hands bumped, their eyes locked.

Rory pulled her hand back as though she'd burned it.

Daniel continued to look at her even as he wrapped his fingers around the handle of the suitcase and lifted it from the truck. "Don't forget to change your bandage," he said as he put it on the ground.

"I won't."

"And if you're still here in two or three days, come to the clinic and I'll take out the stitches for you."

"Thanks."

"Goodbye." He got into his truck without a backward glance and drove away.

Rory watched until he was out of sight. She was used to traveling by herself. She'd been doing it for years. But at that particular moment she felt very alone.

She walked through the screen door of the lobby and approached the reception desk.

The man behind it looked up and smiled. "Hello."

She returned the smile. "Hi. I need a room."

"Of course." He pulled a guest registration book toward him. "For how long?"

"Indefinitely."

"Can you give me an approximation?"

"Two weeks. Maybe three."

"Cash or credit card?"

She opened her purse and took out a credit card. "Is there a place nearby where I can rent a car?" she asked and slid the card toward him across the desk.

"Nearest place would be the airport."

"The one two hours away?"

"Afraid so." He handed her a pen and turned the registration book toward her. "Fill in your name, address and phone number there next to the *x.*"

While she did as he asked, he ran off her credit card and handed it back to her.

"Is there a phone in the room?" asked Rory.

"Yes. And a television." He handed her a key. "You're in Unit 12. To get there, just go out this door and turn right. It's the seventh door down."

"Thanks."

"Do you need some help with your luggage?"

"No, I don't have much."

"There's an ice and soda machine at the end of the building. If you have any problems, just punch zero on your phone."

"All right."

She went outside, lifted her suitcase and walked to her room. The door faced the highway. The room itself was exactly what one would expect. Cheap art on the walls, a bedspread that didn't quite match the drapes. A television bolted to the dresser and a remote control bolted to the bedside table.

It was depressing, but for the time being at least, it was home.

Rory pulled her Day-Timer out of her purse and found the number of the car rental agency. Sinking onto the edge of the bed, she looked at the dialing instructions on the phone and punched in the number. It rang and rang. Someone finally answered.

"Hello," she began. "My name is Rory Milbourne. I rented a car from you yesterday and was involved in an accident."

"Yeah," the woman answered. "We towed it this morning."

"I know. The reason I'm calling is that I need to arrange for another car."

"What kind?"

"Something rugged with a phone."

"Jeep Cherokee?"

"That would be fine."

"Great. We just got one back. I'll get the paperwork done. When will you be in to pick it up?"

"Picking it up is going to be a problem."

"Why?"

"I don't have any way to get there. I was wondering if you could deliver it to me."

"We don't do that."

"I'll pay extra."

The woman sighed at the other end of the line.

Rory sensed an opening. "Look, I wouldn't ask you to do this if it wasn't important. I'm stuck here and I'd really appreciate it if you could help me out."

"All right," the woman said reluctantly. "Technically we're not supposed to do this, but let me see what I can arrange."

"Thank you so much."

"Where are you now?"

Rory gave her the name of the motel. "Room 12."

"Are you going to be there all afternoon?"

"I'll make sure I am."

"Okay. I can't give you an exact time, but I'll send someone as soon as I can."

"Thanks again."

As soon as she hung up from that phone call, she made another one to her office. She was put through to Mary first.

"So you made it in one piece," said the secretary.

"More or less. I had a little accident last night, but I'm fine. Is my uncle in?"

"He just left. He won't be back until tomorrow. Do you want to talk to Bruce?"

She didn't really want to but felt she should. "I guess. Sure. Put him on."

"All right, dear. Just a minute."

While Rory was on hold, she lay back on her bed and stared at the textured plaster ceiling.

Bruce answered without bothering about polite preliminaries. "So, can we start work?"

"No."

"What's going on?"

"Not much. I spoke to Daniel Blackhawk yesterday and today. He's taking a hard line against the mining and has no interest in negotiating a price."

"Let me see if I understand this. You've had two chances to talk Blackhawk into backing off and you weren't successful."

"That's right."

"And you no doubt haven't spoken with Gray Cloud or you would have mentioned it."

"That's right. But I'm going to."

"So to summarize the situation, you've accomplished absolutely nothing since you left here."

She sat up. "No, Bruce, that's not what I'm saying. I've made some contacts and I'm familiarizing myself with the situation. It may take a little time, but I'll get things worked out." She was irritated and it showed in her voice. "And, by the way, were you aware that Daniel Blackhawk is a Harvard-educated doctor of medicine?"

"Yes. So?"

"You might have mentioned it to me."

"What difference does it make?"

"What difference does it make?" she asked in disbelief. "You can't be serious. I came here thinking I was going to be dealing with a man of modest education who'd never been off the reservation. Daniel Blackhawk is neither of those things, and I have to tell you, I don't appreciate that kind of surprise. And he's very sincere in his reasoning for wanting us to not mine on reservation land."

"I don't care who he is or how sincere he comes across. You lay the facts out for him and the rest of his group and tell them to back off."

"They know the facts and they aren't budging. But keep in mind that I've only been here since yesterday afternoon."

"I know, I know. Sorry."

"Thanks, Bruce. This is different from any negotiation I've ever done before. I have to walk before I can run."

"I understand."

"I just called to tell you that things are going to take a little time, but we'll get there."

"I'll pass the word on to my dad."

"Thanks. And tell him I'll call as soon as anything happens."

"Will do."

"Would you put Mary back on the line."

There was a click, followed by a short silence and then Mary picked up the line. Rory asked, "Mary, would you do me a favor and send the portion of the Whispering Pines file that I didn't bring with me?"

"Sure. I think it's in Bruce's office."

She gave her the name of the motel.

"Anything else?"

"In case Bruce forgets, tell my uncle that I'll call him with any news that comes up. If he needs to talk to me in the meantime, the number here is..." She looked at the base of the telephone and read it off. "I'm not going to be able to accomplish much today because of a transportation problem, but tomorrow is another story. I fully intend to go back to the reservation and talk to Gray Cloud, whether his grandson likes it or not."

"I'll give him the message."

"Thanks, Mary."

After she hung up, Rory stayed on the bed, deep in thought.

She was a naturally optimistic person, secure in her abilities as an attorney.

But this situation . . .

She shook her head. This was no time for negative thoughts. She had to be successful. Her uncle had taken her in when he could just as easily have passed her on to someone else. He'd supported her because, as lovely as her parents had been, they were poor as church mice and died deeply in debt. He'd put her through college and law school and had been unfaltering in his love and kindness.

He had always been there for her.

Now, for the first time in her life, it was Rory's chance to be there for him.

Chance? It was her turn. This was the payback.

And whether Daniel Blackhawk wanted it or not, that land would be mined.

Chapter Five

When the last patient had been seen, Daniel walked into the small waiting room where his nurse was filing papers. "Why don't you do that tomorrow, Doris?"

She looked over her half glasses at him. "I'm doing it now precisely so I won't have to do it tomorrow."

Daniel smiled. "Point taken."

She took the glasses off altogether and let them dangle from a gold chain around her neck. "What's wrong?"

"I think I'm just tired."

"Then you should go home and get some rest."

"I will."

"And when was the last time you ate?"

"I had a donut for lunch."

She shook her head. "You're a doctor, for heaven's sake. I shouldn't have to keep reminding you to take better care of yourself. What are these people going to do if you get sick?"

"I don't get sick."

"Through no fault of your own."

Daniel smiled at her and headed for the door. "Don't hang around too long yourself."

"Five more minutes."

Daniel didn't know what he'd do without Doris. She was the lifeblood of the clinic. Because she did her job so thoroughly and so well, all Daniel had to do was be a doctor. Anything else to do with the clinic, anything to do with paperwork, Doris took care of. And mothered him the same way she did her own grown children.

He climbed on his motorcycle and sat there for a moment looking at the clinic. It was his dream to provide really good, up-to-date care for his patients, but money was tight. The equipment he had was certainly functional, but it was old. Most of his patients couldn't afford to pay him with money. They brought muffins or vegetables from their gardens. One of his older patients worked on his motorcycle for free when it broke down. The little money he did get, most of it from the government, went back into the clinic to help with expenses. It just wasn't enough and probably never would be.

Daniel started his motorcycle and rode it to his grandfather's house. The old man was seated in a chair on the porch in near perfect stillness, his eyes closed.

Daniel turned off his machine, put down the kickstand and, after walking up, sat on the top stair of the porch in silence.

A few minutes passed, then the old man opened his eyes and looked at his grandson. "You're troubled," he said.

Daniel nodded.

"Is it the woman?"

Daniel turned his head and looked at his grandfather. "It's strange. When I saw her for the first time yesterday, it was as though I knew her. I didn't understand it. But in the dark hours of this morning, as she lay in my bed, I suddenly realized who she was, and why my feelings for her were—are—so strong."

The old man said nothing.

Daniel needed answers. "Why, all those years ago, didn't you tell me she was white?"

"Her color doesn't matter."

"But it does, Grandfather. All of these years, both on the reservation and away at school, I believed that my destiny was to settle down with a woman of my own kind, to make a home with her and have children. I believed my wife and I would have the common bond of our heritage, the common goal of preserving our important traditions. This woman isn't only white, she's an enemy of our people. She would take what is ours and ruin it."

"And so you sent her away."

"Yes."

"How do you feel?"

"Empty," said Daniel as he gazed into the woods. "Empty in a way that feels as though I'll never be full again."

"Bring her to me, Daniel."

He shook his head. "I'm sorry, Grandfather, but no. I don't want her to come back here."

"And you think what you did this morning will keep her away?" he asked with what appeared to be a smile.

"It was all I could do at the time."

"Your woman is made of much stronger stuff than you give her credit for. You should know that because already, in your heart, you know her better than you'll ever know another human being. She won't leave until all her questions are answered and matters are completely settled. So bring her to me, Daniel. Let me see in person this woman who laid claim to you the night she was born."

Daniel rubbed his forehead. Whether he wanted to admit it or not, he had hoped that his grandfather would deny that Rory was the woman in his vision.

He got to his feet. "I'll get her."

As he rode off, the old man followed his cherished grandson with eyes that, despite the tired skin around them, were startlingly bright and intelligent. He loved Daniel more than life itself. He was more aware than anyone that Daniel carried a certain sadness in his soul. He always had, even as a young child. It wasn't a feeling he inflicted on anyone else. It just was.

For Gray Cloud, to see his grandson genuinely happy would be his greatest joy.

The path to that joy had now arrived in the form of a woman named Rory Milbourne. It remained to be seen if the two of them could wade through the obstacles and find each other.

Rory tossed the shopping bags onto her motel bed and started unloading them. If she was going to be here for a while, she needed to blend in a little better. The business suits she'd brought with her just didn't cut it. The new jeans, shirts and hiking boots should help.

But suddenly she didn't feel very well. She'd done a lot of walking and her head was protesting loudly.

She pushed the clothes to one side, lay down on the bed and closed her eyes. The cut itself was throbbing. She should have picked up some aspirin while she was out.

She'd lain in the darkened room for perhaps an hour when she was awakened by a knock on her door. Rory reluctantly roused herself and went to answer it.

Daniel Blackhawk stood there, his shoulder against the doorframe, his arms crossed over his chest.

Rory was so surprised it took her a moment to find her voice. ''What are you doing here?''

''My grandfather wants to meet you.''

She stepped away from the door to let him come in. ''Why the sudden change of heart?''

''There's been no change on my part. I'm merely following his wishes—against my own better instincts.'' He looked at the clothes scattered across the bed. ''So you're really staying.''

''Yes. I told you I would.''

''I was hoping you'd rethink things.''

''I can't. I have a job to do here.''

He nodded. ''Were you able to get another car?''

''Yes. It's the green one parked outside the room. The rental agency brought it by earlier today. Unfortunately they forgot the phone.''

''Then you'll be able to get around on your own.''

''That's right.''

Daniel sat down in the only chair in the room and waved her onto the bed. ''I need to speak with you about something.''

She turned on a lamp and sat down.

''I know you think of me as being the main obstacle to your mining venture.''

''You and your grandfather.''

Daniel inclined his head. ''What you need to be aware of, if you're going to be driving around the reservation, is that there are those tribe members who are far more militant than those of us who are protesting and blocking the equipment. They won't welcome you any more than they do your workmen. Some of them might be hotheaded enough to take matters into their own hands.''

''So what are you saying?''

''Be careful.''

She was surprised by his warning. ''All right. Thank you for telling me.''

Daniel rose abruptly. "It's going to be dark soon. We should get going."

She rose, also. "Do you want me to follow along behind you in my car?"

"No. I'll take you and bring you back."

"I'll get my purse." She walked around the bed and picked it up from the floor.

As she was following Daniel out, he stopped abruptly and turned. Rory, her thoughts already racing ahead to what she wanted to say to Gray Cloud, crashed into his chest. Daniel's arms went around her and held her in place. For what seemed like an eternity to Rory, but in reality was no more than a few seconds, he looked into her eyes. He raised his hand to her face and lightly rubbed his thumb against her lips, his eyes never leaving hers.

Rory's heart slammed against her ribs. The smallest touch by him seemed to expose her nerve endings. She tingled all over and forgot to breathe. Her lips parted softly in unconscious response.

Daniel couldn't explain what was happening to him. He only knew what he felt. He needed to kiss her and couldn't have stopped himself if he'd wanted to. He lowered his mouth to hers, gently at first, exploring her softness.

Rory's surprise was expressed in her gentle rush of breath as he touched her. Her head told her to pull away, but her body had a mind of its own, and it was too busy reacting to listen. She closed her eyes and savored the way his mouth felt on hers.

Raising his head, he looked into her eyes. "This shouldn't be happening," he said in what amounted to a whisper.

"I know."

Daniel captured her lips again, this time more deeply. He pulled her body close, molding her shape to his.

Rory had no defense. His touch sapped her will. She put her arms around his neck and tangled her fingers in his long hair, drawing him even closer.

He moved one of his hands down the curve of the small of her back and over her gently rounded bottom.

The kiss grew deeper and more searching, setting both of them on fire.

When Daniel finally pulled away from her, he and Rory were both nearly out of control. Another minute and they would have been on the bed.

He turned away from her, his breathing ragged, one hand raised to keep her from talking.

Rory leaned on the chair beside her. Her whole body was shaking. After a minute, Daniel turned back to her. "I'm not going to apologize. It shouldn't have happened, though."

Rory nodded—which was about all the communication she was capable of at the moment.

"Are you all right?"

She nodded again, even though she didn't think she'd ever be "all right" again. One kiss from Daniel Blackhawk and she was changed for a lifetime.

"Let's go," he said, heading for the door.

He mounted his motorcycle while Rory closed and locked the motel room door. When she got behind him, she was reluctant to use his body for balance.

Daniel looked at her over his shoulder. "You have to put your arms around me."

She cautiously scooted forward a little more, until her breasts were pressed against his back, and put her arms around his waist.

A moment later they were on the not very busy highway. It was a fifteen-minute drive to the reservation turnoff, and from there a short ride to his grandfather's.

Rory tried desperately not to feel what she was feeling, but it was nearly impossible with her body pressed up against Daniel's. She remembered having the vague thought yesterday that there was something very sexual about the motorcycle. Well, there was nothing vague about it today.

At one point she tried to loosen her hold, but Daniel caught her hands with one of his and held them in place.

Neither of them attempted to speak above the deep roar of the powerful engine.

But each was very aware of the other's every movement.

When they finally arrived, Gray Cloud was sitting exactly where he'd been two hours earlier. Daniel parked the bike and climbed off. Rory got off quickly so that he wouldn't try to help her. She didn't want him to touch her.

The old man watched as Rory walked toward him. He didn't rise but extended his hand. "Welcome to my home, Miss Milbourne."

She put her soft hand into his work-roughened one and gazed at his still handsome, luxuriously lined face. "Thank you."

Daniel sat on the porch step, his back against a vertical log in the railing, and watched in silence.

I wasn't sure your grandson would even tell you about me."

"Actually," Gray Cloud said with a smile, "I believe it was I who told him about you."

Rory had no idea what he was talking about and didn't ask. What she needed was a polite way of bringing up the mining.

She needn't have worried. Gray Cloud did it for her in his own dignified way.

"I'm told that you are the attorney for the man who wants to dig in our hills."

"That's true."

"You are also his niece."

"Yes."

"That's a strong blood tie," he said quietly, almost to himself. "Tell me, child, what are your thoughts on what your uncle wants to do?"

"Mainly that he has the legal right to mine."

He shook his head. "I asked you for your thoughts, not a legal opinion."

Rory looked toward Daniel for help, but his face was expressionless. She was on her own. "May I sit down?" she asked.

"Of course."

Rory sat in a chair across from him. "I'm sorry, I don't know what to call you."

"Gray Cloud is fine."

"Gray Cloud." She leaned forward and rested her forearms on her legs. "The truth is that I don't know about any of your traditions, legends or beliefs. And I don't know why those particular hills are so important to your people. What I do know is that those who live here are very poor. With the money the tribe would be paid if there is a willingness to negotiate with my uncle—schools could be funded, the clinic modernized. Proper roads could be built. Homes could be repaired and updated. College funding could be supplied to the children who want to continue their education the way your own grandson did. So much good would come of it that the positive qualities seem to me to far outweigh the bad."

The old man nodded. "Believe me when I tell you that I understand what you're saying."

"Thank you. Then perhaps you can explain to me why there's such resistance."

"To do that, you would have to understand our history with the white man and our core beliefs as a people."

"I'm willing to learn. Just tell me what books to get and I'll read them."

"It's not that easy, child. Most of our history has been passed through the generations by word of mouth."

Rory looked at him in surprise. "Are you saying that you don't have a written history?"

"Not a thorough one."

"Then what do I have to do?"

The entire time they'd been talking, the sun had been setting. Gray Cloud now rose. He was surprisingly tall and straight for a man of his age. "You and I will talk again tomorrow."

"Tomorrow?" She hoped she didn't sound as distressed as she felt.

"Yes."

"I was really hoping that we could move things along a little further tonight."

"Don't be so impatient," he said gently. "All will eventually be clear to you. But for now, all God's creatures—particularly his older creatures—should be resting. Good night, Daniel."

Daniel rose as his grandfather walked into his home and closed the door.

And then there were two, thought Rory, as she stood there looking at Daniel.

"What now?" she asked.

"I take you to the clinic to change your bandage and then back to the motel."

She climbed onto the motorcycle and again, reluctantly, put her arms around Daniel.

At her touch, Daniel closed his eyes. Was it possible to experience heaven and hell at the same time?

They rode to the clinic in silence and parked beside a car in the semicircular driveway. Still in silence, Rory followed Daniel inside. There was a pleasantly round middle-aged woman seated behind a worn desk, who looked up with a smile.

"Doris, what are you still doing here?" asked Daniel as he closed the door behind Rory.

"I'm not *still* here. I had some dinner and came back to finish the end-of-the-month paperwork. I think the more interesting question is what are *you* doing here?" Her smiling eyes transferred to Rory.

Daniel took the hint. "This is Ms. Rory Milbourne. She injured her head in an accident yesterday. We came in to change the bandage. Rory, this is Doris Little. She's my nurse, secretary, bookkeeper and dear but nosy friend."

Rory shook the woman's hand, very aware that she was being given the once-over.

"I heard about you," said Doris. "You're an attorney for that mining company."

"Yes."

"Well, I'm not one to meddle in other people's affairs, but I should think there's better use you could put to that degree than what you're doing now." Doris said what she had to, but there was no hostility in her voice.

"There are apparently a lot of people who feel that way," Rory said with a smile.

"Listen to us. We can't all be wrong."

Daniel put his hand in the middle of Rory's back and propelled her toward the door of the examining room.

Doris got up from behind the desk and stood in the doorway to watch. Rory sat on the table as Daniel washed his hands. He looked over his shoulder at Doris. "I thought you had paperwork to do."

The older woman smiled. "I'm sure it'll still be there when I get back to it."

Daniel finished washing his hands then walked to Rory, tilting her face toward his. He held her curls away from her forehead with one hand and removed the bandage with the other.

"How does it look?" she said.

"The way it should."

Rory had the strong feeling he was deliberately not looking her in the eye.

She watched as he went to a white wood cabinet for some salve and a fresh bandage, then walked back to her. "Hold your hair away, please," he asked.

She did.

"Where did you get those curls?" asked Doris. "Your mother or your father?"

"My mom," said Rory with a smile. "She was in a constant battle with her hair."

"Was?"

"Both my parents are dead."

"I'm so sorry," said Doris, coming further into the room. "When did that happen?"

"A long time ago."

Daniel straightened away from her and looked into her eyes. "You were ten," he said quietly.

Rory looked at him in surprise. "Yes, I was, but how do you know that?"

"I just do." He put things away and then helped Rory down from the table.

"Can I fix the two of you some coffee?" asked Doris.

"No, thanks," said Daniel. "I'm going to take Ms. Milbourne back to her motel."

Rory took the hint. "It was nice meeting you, Mrs. Little," she said as she headed out of the examining room.

"Please call me Doris."

"Thank you. I'm Rory."

Daniel was right behind her. "I'll see you in the morning, Doris. If anyone needs me tonight, I'm going straight home after I drop off Ms. Milbourne."

"All right. Good night, you two."

Daniel was already out the clinic door. Rory followed and watched as Daniel climbed onto his motorcycle. "I'm sorry about that," he said to Rory as she climbed on behind him.

"About what?"

"Doris. She's been trying to marry me off for years."

"I think she's wonderful."

"So do I, but I wish she'd leave my personal life alone." With that, he started the engine and they took off.

It was very dark out and, of course, there were no street lamps as they wound their way through the reservation to the main road. Rory was getting used to the motorcycle and didn't hold on to Daniel as tightly as she had been. But her arms were still around him.

Her body was very aware of his.

As he pulled up in front of her motel room door, Rory hurriedly climbed off the back. "Thank you for taking me to see your grandfather. I appreciate it."

Daniel seemed anxious to be off, but he inclined his head.

"What time should I visit him tomorrow?"

"Early."

"All right." She took her room key out of her pocket, inserted it in the lock and turned it.

"Wait!" Daniel was off his motorcycle and behind her.

Rory had been a little startled by his sudden command, but was completely surprised by the way he shoved her to the side and took her place in front of the door.

"What are you doing?"

He turned the key and slowly opened the door. When nothing happened, he turned on the light and opened the door further. Rory came up behind him and looked over his shoulder.

She couldn't believe what she saw. The entire room had been trashed. All of her things were scattered on the floor. Drawers had been pulled out of the dresser and tossed on the floor. The television was smashed. The covers on the bed had been stripped off and left on the floor. The mirror above the dresser had been hit with something that left a spider-web crack spreading out from the center. Scrawled on the glass in lipstick were the words, "Sorry we missed you. Next time we won't."

Rory looked from one point of destruction to another. "Who would do something like this?"

Daniel didn't answer.

Rory bent over and started to pick up her things.

Daniel moved quickly. "You're getting out of here," he said, "right now."

Chapter Six

"What?" Rory asked, startled.

Daniel went to her closet, pulled out her suitcase and started haphazardly throwing her scattered clothes into it. "Look around for anything else you want to salvage."

Doing as she was told, she went into the bathroom and quickly collected her makeup and toiletries. When she walked back into the room, Daniel took the cosmetic bag from her hands and carelessly tossed it into the suitcase, then snapped the lid closed and lifted it off the bed. "Come on."

"Where are we going?" she asked in confusion as she followed him to the door.

"Away from here. Do you have your car keys?"

She pulled them out of the purse she was carrying.

Daniel took them from her and they were out the door. He tossed her suitcase into the Jeep, helped her inside, then walked around to the driver's side and started the engine.

"What about your motorcycle?"

"I'll get it tomorrow. Put on your seat belt."

She glanced at his angry profile as he pulled out of the parking lot. "How did you know someone had been in my room?"

"The window was broken."

"I didn't even notice." She started to ask another question but decided against it. She could literally feel his unwillingness to talk to her at that moment.

Not surprisingly, he turned onto the road heading to the reservation. Rory leaned her head against the back of her seat and watched the miles roll by in the lonely glare of the headlights.

He finally turned down a narrow road and pulled up in front of a home not much larger than his, golden light spilling from all its windows. Daniel hit the horn as he climbed out of the Jeep.

A porch light went on and Jake Troyat stepped outside and narrowed his eyes so he could see who was in the unfamiliar car. "Daniel?"

"Jake," he said, "would you and Susan mind some overnight company?"

"Is Rory with you?"

"Yes."

"Not at all. What's going on?"

While Rory climbed out of the Jeep, Daniel lifted out her suitcase and carried it to the house. "Her motel room was ransacked."

"Did you call the local police?"

"No. My first concern was just to get her as far away from there as quickly as I could."

Jake looked at his friend closely. "Are you saying that you know who did it?"

"I have a pretty good idea."

Susan came to the door, a dish towel in her hand. She smiled when she saw Daniel and smiled even brighter when she saw Rory walking toward her. "What are you two doing here?"

Jake turned to his wife. "Rory needs a place to stay for the night. You don't mind if she stays here, do you?"

"Of course not." She opened the door and ushered Rory inside while Daniel and Jake stayed on the porch talking.

Rory really wanted to hear what the men were saying, particularly since it concerned her, but to do so would have meant asking Susan to stop talking, and Rory just couldn't.

"I understand you met Gray Cloud tonight," said Susan, as she walked through the living room and into the homey kitchen. "What did you think of him?"

"He's intriguing," Rory said, following her. "I'd like to know him better."

"Are you going to see him again?" she asked, standing by the sink.

"Tomorrow morning."

"That's good. He should get to know you, also. Maybe we can ease some of the tension around here." She finished drying off the sink, folded the towel and put it on the counter. "So," she said quietly, looping her arm through Rory's and walking her into the living room, "what's going on?"

"I don't really know, Susan. Daniel barely spoke to me all the way here from the motel."

Daniel and Jake walked in from outside, deep in conversation. A little boy no more than three ran into the room and joyously shouted, "Uncle Daniel!"

Daniel dropped the suitcase just in time to catch the little boy when he hurled himself into Daniel's arms.

Daniel hugged him, and his eyes met Rory's in a long look that didn't go unnoticed by either Susan or Jake.

He put the boy on the ground and tousled his dark hair. "Little Jake. What are you up to?"

Rory watched in amazement as Daniel actually smiled a real smile. Not a half smile, not a little tug at the corners of his mouth. It was a genuine smile.

Little Jake took Daniel's hand and started pulling. "Come with me. I want to show you something."

Her eyes followed them out of the room and for reasons she couldn't begin to fathom, she felt teary.

Susan and Jake looked at each other and smiled the kind of smile that only couples who know each other well understand.

"Come on, I'll show you where you're sleeping," said Jake. He lifted her suitcase and carried it down a short, narrow hallway to what was clearly a child's bedroom. "I hope you don't mind sleeping in the same room as Jake."

"Of course not. It's kind of you to make a place for me so unexpectedly."

He set her suitcase on top of a toy chest.

Rory looked at the back of his head. "Can you tell me what's going on?"

"Daniel just wants to make sure you're safe."

"Safe from what? Who trashed my room?"

Jake turned to face her. "We're not sure. And we're also not sure if they meant you any harm. We just want to be extra cautious."

"Do you think it's the militant group that Daniel told me about?"

"Possibly."

"They might not like the idea of mining, but surely they wouldn't hurt me."

He didn't say anything.

His silence made her nervous. "Would they?"

He looked at her for a long moment. "If they want to make their point badly enough, they just might."

Rory sank onto the edge of the twin bed. Things were going from bad to worse. "So what now?"

"Daniel has a plan."

"What is it?"

"You'll have to talk to Daniel about that."

She sighed.

"Do you want to go back out with me?" asked Jake.

Rory managed a small smile. "I'll join you in a bit. I'd like a few minutes to myself right now."

"Sure."

He left and closed the door behind him. Rory lay back on the bed and stared at the ceiling. In Chicago this had all seemed so simple. She would come to the reservation, successfully negotiate an agreement, return home with good news for her uncle.

Well, there was nothing simple about it. And if anyone had asked her what she really wanted to do at that moment, she would have told them she wanted to go home to her cramped but comfortable little apartment, take the phone off the hook and read a book that had absolutely nothing to do with reality.

Someone knocked on the door.

Rory sat up. "Come in."

Daniel opened the door. "I came to see if you're all right."

"I'm just fine."

"You're only going to be here for one night."

"How considerate of you to let me know that."

Little Jake pushed past Daniel. "I have to go to bed now."

Susan was right behind him. "Sorry," she said with an embarrassed smile.

Rory stood up and looked at her apologetically. "I'm the one who's in the way. I'll just...."

Daniel took her hand. "Come outside with me."

The two of them walked through the house and outside the now-darkened porch. Rory self-consciously pulled her hand from his. "Would you like to tell me what's going on?"

Daniel leaned his shoulder against the house while Rory sat in a wooden rocking chair facing him.

"I didn't like what happened at the motel."

"So you put yourself in charge of my life."

Daniel's eyes rested on her for a long moment. "That's one way of looking at it."

"Is there another?"

Daniel didn't answer. "I brought you here because I knew you'd be safe for the night."

Rory didn't say anything.

"Are you still planning on staying around here indefinitely?"

"Yes."

He looked irritated.

"It's not as though I have a choice."

"All right, all right. If you're going to insist on sticking around, I want you to stay on the reservation itself."

"Why?"

"Because, with my grandfather being in visible and friendly contact with you, you'll be much less likely to be harassed."

"You call doing that kind of damage to my motel room harassment? I just don't understand why anyone would be that upset with me."

His eyes held hers in the moonlight. "Perhaps it's because you want to dig holes in the land of their ancestors."

"And that's worth hurting me?"

"That's worth killing you."

Rory's lips parted softly in surprise. "You're joking."

"I'm deadly serious."

She shook her head. "Great. So where do I go from here?"

"There's a small, abandoned house not far from mine. I'll have it cleaned up for you by tomorrow. You can stay there for as long as you need to, at least until you figure out that there will be no mining on our land."

Rory stopped rocking, but her eyes remained on Daniel. "Why didn't you just leave me at the motel?"

"Maybe that's how things work in your world. It isn't how they work in mine. I may not like who your uncle is or why you're here, but I don't want to see you come to any harm."

Rory got up from the rocking chair. "Well, I just feel warm all over. Thanks." She started to walk past him into the house, but Daniel caught her arm and pulled her back.

"Let go," she said sharply.

"Look," he said, "you know exactly where I stand. I don't want you here. Nobody wants you here. But you have thrust yourself upon us and made yourself our responsibility."

"I didn't ask you to bring me to the reservation. I could just as easily have gone to a different motel. Don't lay your misguided chivalry at my doorstep." She was furious.

"You were found once. You can be found again."

"Then that's my problem." She already felt beholden to him because of her accident. She didn't need this on top of it. She shouldn't have come with him in the first place. "What did you do with my car keys?"

He didn't say anything.

"I want my keys."

"You're not going anywhere."

"Don't tell me what I'm not going to do. Now give me my keys."

"No."

Rory tried to push him away with her free hand, but he caught her wrist and pulled her body toward his.

"Let me go."

"Rory," he said wearily, using her given name for the first time, "stop this."

"I'm not your responsibility."

"As long as you're here, that's exactly what you are."

Rory didn't know why she was so angry. She never got angry.

Daniel pulled her against him and held her stiff and unyielding body in his arms. "Come on," he said softly against her hair. "Relax. This isn't helping anything."

"I know."

"Take some deep breaths."

She did.

"Better?"

"I don't know what's wrong with me. I never behave like this."

Daniel knew.

Her anger drained away.

Daniel could feel her body grow less rigid as he rubbed his hand up and down her back.

She sighed. "Why are you being nice to me?"

"I'm a doctor. I'm nice to all wounded birds."

She raised her head and looked steadily into his dark eyes. "You see me as a wounded bird?"

He pushed her curls away from her face, exposing her bandaged forehead. "At the moment."

What was it about him? Rory wondered as she searched his face. She didn't know him. She didn't know anything about him except that he was the last person in the world she should be showing any weakness to. "I think I should tell you," she said, now calm, "that I don't normally require this much rescuing."

"I'm glad to hear it."

"And I'm also not normally this temperamental."

"I'm doubly glad to hear that."

"And I never ever mix business and—anything else."

"Anything else?" he asked, pulling her closer.

"Ever."

Daniel raised his hand to her face and stroked the smooth skin of her cheek.

"Oh, no," she said helplessly.

His eyes moved over her face like a caress as he pulled her closer in his arms and lowered his mouth to hers.

For Rory, it was happening again. Her mind told her to pull away, but her body refused to move.

It was a wonderful kiss. The kind that didn't lead to anything else. It simply was what it was; gentle and exploring with the kind of promise that left a lovely ache deep inside.

It was a slow kiss with each of them savoring the taste of the other. Daniel kissed the corners of her mouth, then raised his head to look at her. "I would like you, please, to spend the night here," he said with the barest trace of a smile.

She appreciated the "please," as he'd known she would. "Of course I will. And thank you."

He reached into the pocket of his jeans, pulled out the car keys and handed them to her. "You're visiting with my grandfather in the morning. Come to the clinic when you're done and I'll take you to the house you'll be using while you're here."

Both of them suddenly noticed she was still in his arms. Rory stepped back.

"Good night," said Daniel.

She watched while he went down the steps, and continued staring at the same spot long after he'd disappeared along a path in the woods. With a shake of her head, Rory sat on the top step. What was wrong with her? What was she thinking?

She wasn't thinking. That was the problem. Every time the man came near her she turned into someone she didn't know.

It was just that . . .

Rory gave up. There were no words for what she was feeling. But she was going to have to get over it. She would not and could not get involved with Daniel Blackhawk.

Rory got up and walked into the house, closing the screen door quietly behind her. Susan and Jake were in the living room watching television. Jake turned the volume all the way down and smiled at her. "Is everything all right?"

Rory managed a return smile. "Yes."

"Would you like some coffee or anything?" asked Susan.

"No, thank you. I'm really tired. If you two don't mind, I think I'll go to bed."

"Go ahead. We'll see you in the morning," said Jake.

She nodded and walked down the hall to Little Jake's room. He was in the kind of sound sleep that only children can achieve.

In the dim glow of a night-light, Rory searched the rumpled contents of her suitcase, not even sure what was there. She found her blue-and-white cotton trouser pajamas and quietly slipped into them. Susan had turned down the extra bed for her already.

Rory lay down with a weary sigh.

As her eyes drifted closed, the last face she saw was Daniel's.

As Daniel walked to his home, the wolf who came and went fell into step behind him.

Daniel wasn't in a hurry tonight. His movement was weighed down by his thoughts.

When he was alone, it was easy for him to think in terms of reasonable behavior. But when he was with Rory, all of his good intentions disappeared. His mind understood that he should keep his distance. His mind knew that there could only be pain for both of them if things went too far. But the more he tried to push her away, the closer he wanted to draw her to him.

It was a painful pleasure for him to look at her. He wanted to burn her image in his mind so that in the years to come he could call her forth whenever he wanted. He wanted to collect memories of the scent of her, the texture of her skin, the taste of her.

As he came out of the woods, he stood in front of his house and gazed at the lake. The wolf continued on to the cabin and sat on the porch to wait for him.

He wished she'd never come.

Chapter Seven

Rory slept surprisingly soundly and awakened refreshed. She looked across the room and smiled when she saw that Little Jake was still asleep. He was so cute, he almost made her wish she had a child.

Almost.

Rory grabbed a pair of jeans and a shirt out of her suitcase, along with her cosmetic bag, and went down the hall to the bathroom.

After a quick shower and a dash of makeup, she dressed in slim-fitting faded jeans and a billowy blouse tucked in at the waist. Still being as quiet as she could, Rory packed and had her suitcase in her car when Susan came outside, still in her robe.

"Come have breakfast," she said.

"Please don't go to any trouble."

"I'm cooking anyway. What would you like?"

"Whatever you're making is fine."

She followed Susan back inside and into the kitchen and watched as she got out the makings for pancakes. "Can I help?"

Susan handed her a spoon. "Stir."

Rory did just that.

"I understand from Jake that you're going to be staying on the reservation for a while."

"That's the way it looks at the moment. Daniel said something about letting me use a vacant house."

She nodded.

"He's being very nice considering that he disagrees with me completely about the mining."

Susan smiled. "Daniel is a nice man. A good man."

"I know," said Rory quietly.

Susan looked at her discreetly, trying to read her expression.

There was a knock on the screen door. "Hello," called Daniel. "Is anybody up?"

"We're in the kitchen," Susan called back.

Rory's heart gave a little start when he walked into the room. He inclined his head toward Rory and gave Susan a kiss on the cheek.

"You're just in time to have some breakfast with us," said Susan with a smile.

"Thanks. Is Jake up?"

"Up and gone." She took the batter from Rory and ladled it onto a hot griddle. "The local police checked out the hotel last night, but Jake wanted to see it for himself and talk to the manager.''

"Ask him to call me when he gets home."

"Sure."

Rory stood at the counter watching and listening. The atmosphere was so warm and homey.

Little Jake came in, rubbing his eyes with his fists. Daniel picked him up and set him on his lap. The boy leaned against Daniel's chest and sucked his thumb. Daniel rubbed his cheek against Little Jake's silky hair and said something to him in what Rory realized was their native language. The little boy nodded. Daniel asked him something else and then Little Jake answered in the same language.

Susan handed Rory a plate filled with hotcakes. "This is for Daniel," she said.

Rory crossed the kitchen and set the plate in front of him.

"Thank you," he said quietly as he looked up at her.

Susan set down a plate for Little Jake, and Daniel lifted him into the booster seat already on one of the chairs. Two more plates quickly followed and the four of them sat down to eat.

Rory was quiet herself, watching and listening to the others. It was odd, she thought, how completely at home she felt. Susan was like a dear friend she'd known for years.

And Daniel.

She didn't know what to make of her feelings for him. Heart pounding on one hand, comfortable on the other.

Little Jake kept stealing looks at her from under the veil of his long lashes. Whenever she looked back at him and smiled, he would quickly avert his gaze. After a few seconds, he'd look back and they'd do it all over again.

Daniel watched the two of them for a minute, then leaned toward Little Jake. "Are you flirting with the pretty lady?"

He looked at Rory again, smiled and shook his head and dug into his pancakes.

Rory felt another maternal tug and it surprised her. She'd never thought of herself as anyone's mother.

When she looked up and met Daniel's eyes, it was as though he knew exactly what she was thinking. She quickly looked away and didn't look back.

Suddenly ill at ease, Rory quickly finished eating and carried her plate to the counter. "I'll help you clean up."

"Don't be silly," said Susan. "You go on to your meeting with Gray Cloud."

Rory turned, only to find Daniel right behind her with his plate. She looked up at him in surprise. "Oh! Excuse me."

The cloth of his shirt brushed her cheek as he reached around her and put his plate on the counter. He was so close she could smell his clean skin. *Ohh.*

She wasn't even aware that she'd closed her eyes until she opened them again. Daniel had moved away and was looking at her. "I picked up my motorcycle early this morning. Whenever you're ready to leave, I'll show you the way to my grandfather's."

"Thank you. I'm ready now."

Susan stood up and hugged Rory. "I'll probably see you later this afternoon."

"I hope so. Goodbye, Little Jake."

This time he smiled at her. "Bye."

Daniel was already on his way outside. Rory followed him and got into her Jeep at the same time he climbed onto his motorcycle. They were on the road a minute later, Daniel in the lead and Rory following not far behind.

It was a good thing he'd come, she realized, because she would have been utterly and completely lost.

When they finally arrived at the turnoff for Gray Cloud's house just a few minutes later, Daniel pulled to the side of the road and waited for her to stop alongside him.

Rory rolled down her window. "Thanks."

"Where are you going when you leave here?"

"I'm not sure. There are a lot of things I have to do today."

"Be careful. And don't forget to come to the clinic later."

Before she could reply, he roared off.

Rory watched until he was out of sight, then turned down the bumpy dirt road and drove for perhaps a mile before she saw Gray Cloud's house. As she parked in front of it, Rory saw him standing about fifty yards away, gazing out at the lake.

Rory walked up behind him. "Good morning."

He turned his head with its mane of gray hair toward her and nodded. "Let's walk."

Rory was intrigued by Gray Cloud. The man seemed to function on a completely different level than anyone she'd ever met. She unhesitatingly followed him.

They walked in silence down a tree-lined dirt path. Rory knew instinctively not to speak. She had the sense that he was walking much more slowly than he normally did out of deference to her womanhood. Far from being offended, she found it rather charming.

Gray Cloud stopped at a small inlet created by the lake and sat on the ground. Rory sat beside him. As they had approached, the woods reverberated with the noises of animals and insects. And then there was silence—as though someone had flipped a switch.

As Rory and Gray Cloud sat in silent contemplation, the creatures regained their voices. One after the other felt secure enough to interrupt his safe cocoon of silence with noise that grew gradually into a gentle symphony.

Rory wasn't sure how charming she would have found the noises if she'd been alone, but with Gray Cloud there, they seemed friendly rather than frightening.

"Close your eyes," he said gruffly without looking at her. "Really listen."

Rory did. And after a time it was clear that the noises were far from random. It was as though each creature were speaking directly to another, and that creature would answer. Back and forth they went. A smile touched the corners of her mouth. When she opened her eyes, Gray Cloud was watching her. He rose in silence and signaled Rory to do likewise.

Once again they walked. She was grateful for her new hiking boots. But even with them, she seemed to make a lot of noise. Gray Cloud, on the other hand, moved in graceful silence.

Rory's city senses slowly awakened to the natural beauty that surrounded her. The sounds and smells, the play of light and shadow on the trees and the floor of the forest. The path weaved in serpentine fashion around the lake and through the woods.

And then there was a noise she hadn't heard before. It sounded like the rush of water—but not like the lapping of waves. It wasn't anything she'd ever heard before.

Gray Cloud suddenly stopped, raised his face to the sky and closed his eyes.

Rory didn't know what to do, so she just stood there awkwardly, waiting for him to move or say something.

Several minutes passed before he lowered his head, opened his eyes and started walking again. Rory fell in behind him.

The farther they walked, the louder the noise grew.

And then she saw it. A waterfall. It wasn't huge, like Niagara Falls. And it burst from a grassy hill, not a mountain. But it was breathtaking nonetheless. The water hit the narrow, rocky river in a boiling foam that calmed within moments of impact to create a crystal-clear stream.

Gray Cloud and Rory stopped at the edge of the river. The old man took her smooth hand in his callused one, bent over the water and trailed her fingers through its crisp clarity.

"This water is pure," he said, "as is the land around it. It flows into our lake and feeds the springs throughout the reservation, which in turn provide water for the people who live here. The most important thing is to keep the water pure. Natural law tells us this. Common sense tells us this. If we leave nothing else to the future generations who even now watch us from the heavens, we must leave them the land as it came to us."

His eyes met hers to see if she understood. "The mining your uncle proposes to do will ruin the delicate balance Mother Nature and we as her children have tried so hard to keep intact."

Rory had a logical, legal mind. She straightened up and shook the water from her fingers. "I understand your fears. But the mining area is miles away from here. It won't affect your water."

"Everything affects everything else," he said patiently. "Everything is connected. Mining, by its very nature, destroys whatever it touches and drains the lifeblood of the earth."

"I know you don't like the idea of mining but—and I'm sorry if I'm starting to sound like a broken record—we have a legal right."

"What legal right? Yours? Ours? Natural law is far more important than any man's law."

"But man's law is the one that can be enforced. Please believe me, Gray Cloud, when I say that I don't want to do anything to hurt anyone. But I have my uncle's interests to protect and I'll do what I must to see that they are."

"Including having us arrested on our own land."

"No one has done that."

"Not yet, but the threat is there."

"You have my word of honor that nothing like that will happen. We want to work with you, not against you."

He looked at her for a long time. "Are you aware that we, as a tribe, were given this land to use as our own more than two hundred years ago?"

"Yes."

"Are you also aware that we were given the word of your government that they would not interfere with our use of the land in any way that we saw fit?"

"Yes. But the land doesn't actually belong to your tribe. It belongs to the government. And if the government wants to mine on the land, it has that right."

"Your government gave us their word that our sacred hills would remain as they are and have always been."

"I didn't see any papers that said that."

"It was a spoken trust."

"But there's no proof. For heaven's sake, that was nearly two hundred years ago."

"Does that make it any less valid?"

"If there's no one alive who witnessed this spoken trust, yes."

"Our proof is our word."

Rory was at a loss. She believed him. At least she believed that he was sincere, but a claim like that would not have a chance in a court of law.

And that left her squarely on the right side of the law as far as mining the hills was concerned.

So why wasn't she happier?

Because it didn't feel right, she thought, answering her own question. "I'd like to avoid taking this to court."

"What do you suggest?"

"Negotiation. We give you money, you allow us access to the hills for mining." She studied him for a long moment. "If there's a court battle, we'll win."

Gray Cloud was silent for such a long time that Rory thought he'd forgotten she was there. And then he spoke.

"I understand from my grandson that you intend to stay here on the reservation."

"With your permission," she said politely, recognizing that very little happened on the reservation without it.

"You have it, of course."

"All I'm asking for is a chance to present my case for mining before you and the rest of your tribe and explain what we would like to see in the way of shared profits."

"They won't agree to it."

"Perhaps. Perhaps not. I can be very persuasive."

"So I see."

For the first time since arriving on the reservation, Rory actually felt a little hopeful.

Gray Cloud inclined his head in the direction from which they'd come. "Let's go."

It was a long walk back, but Rory didn't mind. She was developing an entirely new awareness of her surroundings.

So much so that she knew she was being followed.

She turned her head and looked behind her.

The wolf was there, perhaps twenty feet away.

Rory kept walking. She was a little uneasy, but certainly not as frightened as she'd been the first time she'd seen him.

Gray Cloud stopped walking. Rory stopped right behind him. She turned to look at the wolf and found that the animal had also stopped and was watching them.

Then Gray Cloud started walking again, and Rory and the wolf followed.

When they got to his house, he surprised Rory by not inviting her inside. Instead, he turned to her and, with an almost regal inclination of his head, wished her a good afternoon and disappeared inside.

He'd said nothing about her request to speak to the tribe.

She stood there for a few minutes, thinking that he might come back out, but he didn't.

Rory turned to see what the wolf was doing and found that he was gone.

Poof.

Feeling a little odd at the way the visit had ended, Rory got into her Jeep, turned it around and left the same way she'd arrived. When she got to the main road, she turned right and headed for the motel so she could call her uncle, and also to see if the file Mary had couriered to her had arrived.

This time she found her way through the reservation without any trouble. It seemed to have only one main road that cut right through it. If you knew what turnoffs to take from the main road, you could get anywhere.

When she got to the motel, Rory pulled up in front of the office and went inside. The same man who'd checked her in the day before greeted her with something less than enthusiasm. She managed a tentative smile. "I'm sorry about what happened yesterday."

"Not half as sorry as I am. Of course, I'm glad to see that you're all right, but the damage is going to cost me hundreds of dollars."

"Won't your insurance cover it?"

"Some. Not all. I still have to fork over the five-hundred-dollar deductible."

Rory felt really bad. The motel wasn't much to speak of, but it was the man's business and probably all he had. She pulled out her checkbook.

"Oh, no," he said with a shake of his head, when he saw what she intended. "It's not your fault. It's nobody's fault, except the vandals who did the damage.

Rory finished writing, ripped out the check and put it on the counter. "I might not have done it myself, but it happened because of me. I owe you at least the deductible. If the police ever catch the people responsible, they can pay me back. Fair enough?''

He didn't exactly smile, but his expression lightened.

''By any chance, did a package come for me today?''

He pulled a six-inch-deep box out from under the counter. ''It was just delivered about an hour ago.''

''Thanks,'' she said and slipped it under her arm. ''And is there a phone I can use?''

''Outside by the soda machine.''

''Thanks.''

Rory tossed the box into her Jeep and walked down the row of rooms to the end. She made the call collect and waited for someone at the other end to accept the charges. She got the receptionist, then Mary and then her uncle.

''Tell me you have good news,'' he said, not wasting time on conversational preliminaries.

''I wouldn't call it good. I think *hopeful* is a better word.''

''Go on.''

''There was an incident at the motel I was staying at last night. Blackhawk invited me to stay on the reservation for the duration of my visit and Gray Cloud gave the offer his okay this morning.''

''I still haven't heard anything hopeful.''

''This gives me a chance to get to know the people better. Once I can understand what their thinking is,

I'll have a better chance of negotiating a compromise.''

"I don't have time for this, Rory."

"It's the best I can do at the moment. These people won't negotiate. Perhaps you weren't aware of it when you started this, but those hills are sacred to them. Daniel Blackhawk referred to our presence there as an invasion.''

"It's all nonsense."

"To you, but not to them. And Gray Cloud told me today that there was a spoken agreement made more than two hundred years ago that those hills would be allowed to remain as they were then. Did you know anything about that?''

"I heard something about it," he said dismissively. "But as far as I can tell, it's nothing more than a rumor. There's absolutely no evidence to back up the claim.''

"I told him that."

"We could clean the tribe's clock in court."

"I phrased it a little differently, but I told him pretty much the same thing.''

"What did he say?"

"What could he say? He stands firmly by what he believes to be the truth.''

"And Blackhawk?"

"He pretty much dared us to take them to court. He knows as well as anyone that we don't have that kind of time. I think he figures by the time the case makes it onto the actual court docket, we'll have gone bankrupt. Problem solved.''

"He's right."

"I know."

There was a long silence. "What's next?"

"I stay here, mingle, learn about their customs and beliefs and try to approach them about the mining in a way that's consistent with something that won't offend them."

"You could be there for months."

"Weeks."

There was a long pause. "I guess you should try it your way. But if it doesn't work, I'll have to look at other options."

"Such as arresting them?"

"That's right. Press or no press, something has to be done."

"I gave Gray Cloud my word that we wouldn't do that. I told him that we wanted to work with him, not against him."

He sighed. "Don't get us boxed in, Rory."

"I'm just trying to work according to their rules."

"All right," he finally said. "Go ahead and stay there. But keep me posted. I want to know absolutely everything that's going on. Is there anything else?"

The thought that she should tell him what had happened to her motel room last night crossed her mind, but she brushed it aside. There was no point in worrying him about something he could do nothing about.

"No. I'm going to try to get back to the site sometime today to see how things are going there."

"Anything new on that front?"

"No. We have people, they have people."

"Did you meet Joe McDermott?"

"Yes, and I can't say that I much liked him."

Her uncle laughed. "I'll admit that Joe is a little rough around the edges, but he's an all-right guy. You're just not used to workingmen."

"I've met my share of 'workingmen' as you call them, and none of them has made my skin crawl the way Joe does."

"Well, get used to it, because you two are going to be working closely together."

"In what capacity?"

"He's the foreman, Rory."

"I know. What does that have to do with me?"

"Plenty. He has to be kept apprised of everything that's going on. And by the same token, he's supposed to keep his eyes and ears open and keep you informed."

"I don't think he's all that reliable."

"I do, and he works for me."

"Yes, sir." Every ounce of women's intuition in her told her that the man was bad news from start to finish.

"Rory?"

"I'm still here."

"We play at least part of this my way."

"I know."

"You may be my niece, but it's my company."

"I understand."

"And I want you to keep in your mind at all times exactly how important this is to all of us. If this deal doesn't go through, it's the end of everything."

"I'll do my best," she said quietly. "That's all I can do."

When Rory hung up the phone, she stood there for a few minutes deep in thought. She didn't feel optimistic at all.

She wished her uncle didn't have so much riding on this one deal. He may well have met his match in Gray Cloud.

And she may well have met hers in Daniel Blackhawk.

Chapter Eight

Rory climbed back in her Jeep and drove to the clinic. The area in front was filled with cars. She parked off to one side and sat there, not really sure what to do. She glanced at her watch. Four o'clock. Maybe she should go to the mining site first and then come back here so Daniel could show her where she'd be staying.

The solution to that minor dilemma was reached when Doris stepped into the doorway and waved at her to come in.

Rory slipped her keys out of the ignition and, leaving her purse and everything else in the Jeep, locked it and went into the clinic.

The chairs lined up against the wall held mostly mothers and children. There were only a couple of men.

All eyes seemed to follow Rory as she crossed the room to Doris.

"Daniel is going to be at least another hour," said Doris. "If you're going to be waiting for him anyway, I thought maybe I could put you to work."

"Sure. What would you like me do do?"

Doris smiled. "I love people who ask questions like that." She handed Rory an armload of files. "These go in the second cabinet, top drawer. Alphabetize them by last name."

Rory carried them across the room, aware of being watched. She didn't know whether to ignore it or acknowledge it. So she did a little of both by looking at a person here and a person there and smiling at them as she filed. There were a few smiles in return, but not many. Word had apparently gotten out.

Daniel came out of the examining room for his next patient and saw Rory. He and Doris had a quiet thirty-second conference. Then, to Rory's surprise, Daniel walked over to her and put his hand at her waist protectively as he turned her completely toward the waiting room. "Everyone," he said, "as I'm sure most of you already know, this is Rory Milbourne. She's here representing the mining company that wants to do work in our hills. My grandfather and I have invited her to stay here for as long as she cares to. We hope all of you will try to make her feel welcome, regardless of how you feel about the mining."

There were still some who didn't look happy, but there seemed to be a lessening of the hostility.

Daniel gave her waist an encouraging squeeze, then dropped his hand and walked away from her. He stopped in front of some of the children, hunkering down in front of them so they were eye level, and asked them questions about how they were feeling. It was clear to Rory that the children and parents thought the world of Daniel. He picked up one child and carried her into the examining room as the mother followed behind.

Rory watched until the door closed behind them. As she looked away, she caught Doris's eye. The older woman smiled knowingly and went back to her paperwork.

By the time Rory had finished her filing, Daniel was down to his last patient. Rory sat on one of the chairs and waited.

When he finally came out, Doris pushed some papers across the desk toward him. "You're not going to step so much as a foot out the door before you sign these."

And so he did, page after page after page.

When he was finished, Doris handed him a palm-size black beeper. "Don't forget this."

"You use a pager?" Rory asked in surprise.

"We gave up smoke signals about ten years ago," said Daniel, not looking at her as he pocketed it.

Rory didn't say anything. She knew a verbal smack when she heard it.

"How did your meeting with my grandfather go?" he asked, still shuffling papers.

"It was—interesting."

"Because?" he prompted.

"I've never met anyone like him." She looked at him curiously. "You already know how it went, don't you?"

"I spoke with him briefly this afternoon." Daniel looked at Doris, who had been discreetly listening at her desk. "What do you think, Doris? Are we letting ourselves in for all kinds of trouble by taking the enemy to our bosom?"

"Is it all right with your grandfather?" she asked.

"He gave his permission."

"Then we're doing the right thing," pronounced Doris. "Your grandfather is a wise man. He always knows what he's doing. You can't go against him."

"Just a minute," said Rory. "I'm not the enemy. I'm not here to hurt anyone. I'm here to help."

Daniel glanced at Doris once more as he handed her the pen. "Money again," he said.

Doris shook her head. "The root of all evil."

"Money can be used for wonderful things. I really don't understand this aversion to financial security that I keep hearing," Rory said, more to herself than to them.

"There's nothing wrong with financial security," said Daniel. "But you shouldn't make that your main focus in life. There are other things so much more important."

"Not if you don't have it."

Daniel signaled her to get up. "Come on. I'll take you to the house where you'll be staying."

She looked at Doris as she stood up. "It was nice seeing you again."

"Thanks for the help."

Rory followed Daniel outside. She climbed into her Jeep and he onto his motorcycle.

They followed the main road for a few minutes, then veered off onto a driveway of sorts that led to a very small cabin. It was set slightly back from the water and seemed from the outside to be quite a bit smaller than Daniel's, with a porch running only on the side of the house that faced the lake.

Rory parked behind Daniel and went with him inside.

The first thing Rory noticed was how clean it was. And even though it was set in the woods, the same sunlight that filtered through the trees peeked through the curtains. There was a four-poster bed with a beautiful quilt done in earthy colors. She also saw a fireplace, a refrigerator and a stove—all the amenities anyone could ask for. Rory hadn't expected to be charmed, but she was. "This is really nice."

"Susan and some others worked hard today to clean it up for you. I'm sure you'll find whatever you need in the refrigerator."

"Thank you."

"My house is about three hundred yards down the path. If you need anything, ask."

"All right. Do I pay rent?"

"You're our guest. Of course you don't pay rent."

"Can I at least pay for the food?"

"Not for what's here now, but for whatever else you need, you'll have to."

Rory didn't say anything further about it, but she really felt terrible. They had so little and she had so much. She didn't feel right about accepting this kind of hospitality.

But she also knew when it was time to let something drop. Daniel's tone made it abundantly clear that now was the time. She looked around the cabin.

"What now?" she asked.

"Unpack. Settle in."

"And then what?"

"Do what you need to satisfy yourself with the situation one way or another and then leave."

Rory watched him with almost clinical fascination. Last night they'd kissed. Tonight it was as though they were strangers.

Daniel turned to look at her and once again she had the uneasy feeling that he knew exactly what she was thinking. His eyes moved to her mouth and rested there briefly—but long enough for her to understand that he hadn't forgotten anything. "If there isn't anything else you need, I'll be going," he said.

"Are you coming back?"

"You're on your own, Rory. What you do with your time from here on out is up to you. I'm not your caretaker."

"No, I know that. You just caught me a little off guard."

He headed out the door. "If you get a chance, stop by the clinic tomorrow and I'll take out your stitches."

"All right," Rory said as she followed him out.

Without even a wave, he got on his motorcycle and took off.

Yep. That was it. Of course it wasn't his job to entertain her. She was the one who had decided to stay.

She looked back into the cabin, feeling a little lost. Nothing to do in there. So she sat on the porch.

Woods on three sides of the cabin, water on one.

She felt surrounded—and not in a warm, secure way.

Busy. She'd keep herself busy.

Leaving the porch, she went to her car for her luggage. While she was there, she grabbed her purse and the package from Mary and carried everything inside. There was an old-fashioned dresser with bright but faded paint that probably would have fetched a fortune at an auction. She neatly arranged whatever didn't need hangers in the drawers. There was no closet, but there was an armoire of sorts, also old and very lovely in its own way, with some empty hangers already on the rod. There were also loose papers from the file she'd brought with her and had once been scattered throughout her motel room. She put those on a desk in the corner to sort through later.

When she'd finished unpacking, she found the bathroom and looked inside. It was small, with an interesting shower that had a clear ceiling to let the sunlight in.

Out of idle curiosity, she turned on the tap. Sure enough, hot water.

She spotted a small bookshelf in a corner of the living room and tilted her head to one side to read the titles. There were some novels, but most of the books had to do with something pertaining to Native Americans.

She picked out one that looked interesting, sat in a comfortable chair and began to read.

Perhaps an hour had passed when there was a knock on the door.

"Hello!" called Susan as she peered through the screen.

Rory couldn't put the book down fast enough. She nearly knocked her chair over getting out of it. "Hi!" she said happily as she opened the door. "What are you doing here?"

"I wanted to make sure you were settled in." She looked around. "How do you like it?"

"It's wonderful. Thank you for going to the trouble of getting it ready. Daniel told me you helped."

"Daniel talks too much. And it wasn't just me. Several of us worked on it."

"Thank them for me, too."

"I will. Are you sure you have everything you need?"

"Positive."

"And you know where the grocery store is?"

"Yes. I stopped there on my first day."

Susan walked over to the bed and smoothed a wrinkle in the cover. "Jake went to the motel this morning."

"I knew he was going to. Did he find out who did it?"

"No. But he found out who didn't do it."

Rory looked at her curiously.

"It wasn't the militant among us. It wasn't any of us."

"Then who?"

"No one knows. Or if they do, they aren't talking."

"Did Jake tell Daniel?"

"Probably not yet. Jake's on duty tonight and Daniel is working with the protestors."

"Daniel?" asked Rory in surprise.

"Everyone takes a turn. We do it in shifts."

Rory smiled. "Your protest sounds very organized."

"We have different shifts three times a day, seven days a week."

"That must take a lot of planning."

"Not really. Everyone knows when it's his or her night to be there."

"How many people at one time?"

"Never fewer than five. Even at that we can't outnumber yours, but we try to make a constant showing." She looked at her watch. "I have to go home. Little Jake is waiting for his dinner. I have to pick him up at my mother's. I just wanted to make sure you got settled in all right." She hugged Rory. "We'll probably see each other tomorrow."

"Thanks again, for everything."

Rory stood on the porch and waved as Susan drove off.

Alone again.

She sat on the top step and watched as the sun dropped lower and lower in the sky. When night fell, it was the blackest place she'd ever been.

And there were the noises again. The night noises were different from the day ones. Not as friendly.

Not friendly at all.

She heard a wolf howl in the distance. Moments later another one answered.

Rory nervously got up from the step and went inside the cabin, flicking on every light switch she could find until everything was bathed in a golden glow.

This wasn't good. Not good at all.

She heard another howl. This one sounded closer. She went to the door, latched the screen and shoved the solid door closed after it.

There. Now she'd be safe. Besides, the evening was cool. It was almost too cool to leave the door open.

How was that for rationalizing?

Rory poked through the refrigerator. There was a lot of food, but eggs looked good to her for some reason. She found a skillet and a spatula and went to work frying a couple of them and browning some toast.

As she ate at the little table, she continued reading the book. It was fascinating. She realized that what little knowledge she had of Native Americans was largely of the Plains, not Woodland tribes. The art of the Woodland Indians was rooted in the colors and shapes of things found in a forest while the others' art tended to look more geometric.

When she'd finished eating, she cleaned up the kitchen, then went to the desk and began to organize the messy file. Paper by paper, she read as she organized.

The more she read, the more she wished she had access to any case law that pertained to the government allowing mining on tribal land without the tribe's permission. And even at that, the case law might not be that helpful. What she really needed to look at were the treaties between the tribe and the government. All of the treaties.

But...

Frankly, that was something the tribe itself should do if they wanted to defend themselves in court against the mining. Her job was to represent her uncle's corporation, not look for loopholes for the tribe.

She got tired early. It wasn't even nine o'clock when she went into her bathroom, scrubbed her face, brushed her teeth and got ready for bed.

Bed, she thought with a sigh, as she sank onto the soft mattress and pulled the covers up over her. She had to admit that she enjoyed sleeping more than she used to.

The lights were still on.

She could have gotten up to turn them out.

Nah.

Maybe they'd scare off whatever was outside.

She lay there for a time, trying to fall asleep and unable to, yet reluctant to get up.

Then she heard sounds coming from the porch. Footsteps. And some kind of scratching noise. She thought about her motel room and the message on the mirror.

Suddenly she was wishing she'd turned out the lights. Darkness was her friend, not her enemy.

Dashing out from under the covers, she hit every switch until the cabin was engulfed in darkness. Walking on tiptoe to one of the windows that faced the porch, she carefully lifted the curtain and looked outside. There was just a little sliver of moon peeking out from behind the clouds. Not really enough to do any good.

At first she didn't see anything.

And then she spotted the wolf. He was sitting at the top of the stairs, looking out toward the lake. His head was up. His body language told her he was on alert.

Rory put her hand over her hammering heart and willed herself to calm down. Everything was all right. The wolf had come to watch over her. Maybe Daniel was right after all about the wolf turning himself into her protector.

With a smiling shake of her head, Rory went back to bed, this time leaving the lights off. It was only a matter of minutes before she was sound asleep.

And she stayed that way until the middle of the night when someone started pounding on the door.

Chapter Nine

Rory sat straight up, instantly and completely awake.

"Open the door!" yelled Susan.

Rory turned on the bedside lamp and ran to the door. The woman nearly fell into the cabin. "You have to do something."

"About what?"

"Daniel and Gray Cloud have been arrested."

"What?"

"Both of them were at the mining site tonight and they were arrested along with everyone else who was there."

"By whom?"

"The police."

"Tribal?"

"Good heavens, no. City."

"On whose authority?"

"I don't know," she said breathlessly. "I just know that some man who works for the same corporation as you was there orchestrating the whole thing."

Rory went to her drawers and pulled out some clothes. "Do you have a name?" she asked as she hurriedly put on some jeans and a sweater.

"Just a first one. Bruce."

Rory stopped in midmotion. "Bruce?"

"Yes."

"Oh, no."

"Do you know him?"

"He's my cousin."

"What's he doing here?"

"I don't know, but you better believe I'm going to find out." She grabbed her purse and car keys. "Where is everyone now?"

"Still at the site the last I heard, though they may have been taken to jail by now."

"Do you know if my cousin is still at the site?"

Susan shook her head.

"We'll go there first."

"Follow me," said Susan. She hurried out the door with Rory following. "It's hard to find in the dark."

Rory saw a flash of lightning and heard thunder rumbling in the distance. Perfect.

With headlights their only illumination, the two of them drove the winding roads of the reservation toward the hills.

Rory's heart sank as they pulled into the mining area. The crew—a different shift from the men Rory had seen before, except for the obnoxious foreman— were lined up and yelling at handcuffed members of the tribe. The press was there in full force with their bright television lights flooding the entire area.

Rory jammed the gearshift into Park and jumped out of her car. Susan was right behind her.

Bruce was there, speaking into a microphone a reporter had thrust in his face. He was obviously angry, jabbing a finger toward the protestors and yelling above the noise of the crew. Rory had to force herself to appear calm when in fact she was raging on the inside. She grabbed his shoulder and squeezed so hard her fingernails dug into his skin. Then she smiled tightly at the reporter. "Excuse us, please."

The woman doing the interview shoved the microphone into Rory's face. "Who are you?"

Rory brushed it aside with the back of her hands. As she turned her head away, she saw Daniel. He was standing absolutely still, his eyes on her, his hands cuffed in front of him. Gray Cloud stood beside him, his hands also cuffed.

Even angrier, she grabbed Bruce, who had to weigh a hundred pounds more than she did, and dragged him to her car and out of the earshot of reporters. "What the hell do you think you're doing?" she asked furiously, trying in vain to keep her voice low.

"Moving things along," he said without apology. "I got a call from Joe earlier today telling me that some of the protestors had damaged our equipment. If they want to play those games, I'll have them arrested, and they're going to stay arrested until they make restitution."

"How could they have possibly damaged anything with our crew here watching over everything?"

"All I know is that the land mover and drills have been sabotaged and the only people who have an interest in doing something like that are standing over there in handcuffs."

Rory got hit on the cheek by a large drop of rain, but she was so angry she didn't notice.

"They wouldn't do that."

Bruce looked at her in surprise. "Well, you certainly seem to have become knowledgeable about this tribe all of a sudden."

"These are honorable people."

"The machinery is damaged. How would you explain it?"

"I can't. And unless you have an eyewitness, neither can you."

The rain began to fall in earnest in big drops that stung when they hit bare skin.

"It sounds to me as though you've forgotten who you work for," said Bruce.

"I know exactly who I work for and what I'm here to do. Which brings me to another point. What are you doing here?"

"I told you. Joe called me."

"Why didn't he call me?"

"He couldn't find you. You weren't at the motel last night or this morning." His tone was suggestive.

"I had to leave. My room was ransacked."

"Let me guess," he said. "These honorable people had nothing to do with that, either."

She had no answer, only questions. "Does your father know you're here?"

"Of course he does."

"Does he know you're doing this?"

"Not specifically. He knows I'm here to help you out."

"Well, you're not helping. Go home, Bruce."

"I think you're forgetting whose deal this is. I found the site. I got government approval. I purchased the machinery and I hired the crew. This is my baby, not yours."

"And Uncle Bill sent me to negotiate."

"Your idea of negotiation appears to be letting Blackhawk and Gray Cloud lead you around by the nose without even agreeing to sit down with you for serious discussions. I don't think so, Rory."

"I've only been here for a couple of days, Bruce. This is going to take time. I have to win their confidence. How am I going to do that with you showing up here and leading these people off in handcuffs?"

"Rory, they've broken the law and cost us tens of thousands of dollars in damages. Don't you see what an opportunity this is? We arrest them now and we start work tomorrow."

"The people you're arresting are going to be instantly replaced with others."

"Then we'll have them arrested, too."

"Bruce, please trust me on this. I know what I'm doing. You tell the authorities to let these people go this minute. If you don't," she threatened, "I'll personally go to the jail and bail them out."

Lightning split the sky and the thunderclap that followed shook the earth. Rory didn't notice.

"You wouldn't," said Bruce.

"Oh, but I would, and you know it. And if that doesn't stop you, I'll file an injunction."

"You really have forgotten whose side you're on, haven't you?"

"I haven't forgotten anything, Bruce. What you don't seem to understand is that the way this is handled is every bit as important as the end result."

"So you're going to let them get away with this?"

"I'm not convinced they did it."

"Who else has a motive?"

"I don't know." She shook her head. "I just don't know, but you can bet I'll look into it."

"That's comforting," he said sarcastically. "I'm sure Dad will appreciate your integrity when he files for bankruptcy."

Rory refused to let him change the subject. "I want those people let go and I want them let go now. Do you understand?"

Bruce clenched his fists. For just a moment, Rory thought he might actually hit her, the way he had when they were children, but she stared him down. As he turned on his heel and strode away, she let out a long, shaky breath and watched as he walked to one of the police officers. For the most part, Bruce was a reasonable man. But there were times when his temper frightened her.

She shifted her attention to the foreman, who was standing about ten feet away. She planted herself in front of him. "What happened?" she asked.

He shrugged. "You know what I know."

"If you believe these people sabotaged the machinery, how do you think they got to it with you and your men watching over it?"

"You know Indians. They can sneak up behind you without making a sound." He made a slicing motion with his fingers across his throat.

Rory didn't even have to think about what she said next. "You're fired."

He grunted a short laugh of disbelief. "I don't work for you. You can't fire me."

"I just did."

"You don't have the authority."

"Pick up your check at the mining company office tomorrow. I find you here again, I'll have you arrested."

"We'll see what Bruce has to say about this."

"You can talk to him all you want, as long as it's nowhere near here."

He gave her a steady, dark look and walked away.

Susan and Jake moved to stand on either side of her. Jake's wary eyes followed the bulky foreman. "What's going on?" he asked.

"I spoke to my cousin. He's talking to the police now and telling them to let everyone go."

"I mean with that guy."

"I just fired him."

"He's bad news."

Rory nodded absently. She knew she'd done the right thing, but Joe McDermott's final look stayed with her. She glanced up at Jake. "I'm sorry about all this."

"It's not your fault."

Susan caught Rory's hand and held it in her own. "We understand that you weren't behind this."

She appreciated the support, but it didn't really help. She watched a policeman as he made his way to the handcuffed men and women. One by one he unlocked them. Gray Cloud and Daniel both looked straight ahead as their hands were freed. And even after the handcuffs had been removed, they stood there unmoving.

Jake gave Rory's shoulder an encouraging squeeze then went to his friend.

Reporters were rushing around in the downpour. They questioned both Blackhawk and Gray Cloud. Neither man responded; neither man even acknowledged the presence of the cameras or reporters.

And Daniel, after that first moment when she'd arrived, hadn't looked at Rory again.

Jake signaled Susan to come to him, but she was reluctant to leave Rory. "Are you going to be all right?" she asked.

"I don't know. I feel as though I should say something to Daniel and Gray Cloud."

"Now isn't the time. Wait until tomorrow when tempers have cooled. Now answer my question. Are you all right?"

Rory nodded and managed a smile.

Susan kissed her on the cheek. "We'll talk tomorrow."

No sooner had Susan walked away than Bruce came back to her. "You've made me look like a fool."

"You did that all by yourself."

"My dad isn't going to be happy."

"Oh, Bruce," she said tiredly, "you sound like a little boy who has to share his toys."

"This is my project."

"So you keep reminding me." She pushed her dripping wet curls out of her face. "Are you going back to Chicago now that you've managed to wreak havoc here?"

"Not a chance. Someone needs to keep an eye on you."

"Do you honestly believe that anyone here is going to be willing to negotiate if you're within a hundred yards of them?"

"Get used to it, Rory. I'm not going anywhere."

Rory walked away from him and went to her car. With an angry roar of her engine, her headlights slicing the night, she spun her tires a moment before they caught and she took off.

She had no trouble finding her way home. When she got there, she cut the ignition but stayed in the car and listened absently to the rain pelting it. Her thoughts ran all over the map, flitting from one place to the other so quickly that everything came to her in a jumble.

With a shake of her head, she climbed out of the Jeep and walked to the house. She didn't want to go inside, so she stayed on the porch, pacing back and forth in the dark.

She had to talk to Daniel. She had to apologize.

He'd said she could find him down the path, so she took off walking in the rain, lightning flashing overhead.

Light shone from his windows. Rory stopped on the edge of the path and stared at the house. Should she or shouldn't she?

She had to.

Gathering her nerve, she crossed the yard and walked up the steps, knocked and waited.

A woman opened the door.

The surprise momentarily robbed Rory of her voice. She was lovely and clearly Native American.

"Yes?" the woman prompted.

Rory cleared her throat. "Excuse me. I wanted to speak to Daniel, but I can see that I'm interrupting."

Daniel, still wet from the rain and wearing only his jeans with a towel around his neck, stepped into view. "What do you want?"

She felt uneasy. She didn't know why she hadn't expected him to be involved with someone. He was a perfectly healthy man. It didn't have anything to do with her.

So why did it bother her so much?

She tried to behave as though it didn't. "Nothing. I'll talk to you tomorrow." She turned and headed down the steps.

"Wait," said Daniel.

She turned back, still standing in the rain.

The other woman looked from one to the other. "Well," she said suddenly, "I was just leaving anyway." She grabbed an umbrella that rested in a corner of the porch and passed Rory as she went down the steps to a car that Rory hadn't noticed earlier.

Daniel stood in the doorway. "Come in out of the rain," he said quietly.

"I can talk to you from here."

"Don't be ridiculous. Come inside."

"No."

Daniel didn't push her, but stood in the doorway and watched as the rain ran down her face.

"I'm sorry for interrupting."

"You didn't. Jane is a good friend, nothing more."

"You don't have to explain. It's none of my business."

"Rory..."

She looked at him through the rain. "I came here to apologize for what happened in the hills. I gave your grandfather my word that no one would be arrested."

"It wasn't your fault."

"I intended going to the hills tonight. I should have done it. If I had, I would have known that my cousin was there." She looked away from him. "Anyway, I'm sorry." She turned to leave.

"Rory," called Daniel, "come in out of the rain."

She shook her head and walked quickly away from him.

Daniel came off the porch after her.

As soon as Rory realized he was behind her, she broke into a run. She didn't know why she was running; she just knew she couldn't be with him at that moment.

Daniel tackled her from behind, breaking her fall by turning so that his body was the one that hit the ground with Rory on top of him.

"What are you doing?" she yelled, struggling against him.

Daniel flipped her over so that she was on her back and he was on top of her. "The question is, what are you running from?"

"I was just trying to get home."

"I don't think so. You were trying to get away from me. Why?"

"I was embarrassed."

"Try again."

She stopped struggling and looked at him. "I don't know."

He pushed her wet curls out of her face. "Are you afraid of me?"

"No," she said.

Daniel lowered his mouth to hers and kissed her with a tenderness that left an ache in her soul. As he raised his head and looked into her eyes, she saw pain in his expression. "The first night you were here," he said, "I promised myself that I wouldn't allow anything to happen between us."

Her eyes moved over his face. "And now?"

"I didn't expect to feel..." He stopped himself from finishing the sentence. "I didn't expect this."

"I know."

"So here we are," he said, "a conflict of interest waiting to happen."

"What should we do?"

In answer to her question, Daniel lowered his mouth to hers and kissed her so deeply she felt it run through her entire body.

He pushed himself away from her and stood up. Then he took her hand and pulled her against him. "You're staying with me tonight." Lifting her in his arms, he carried her inside the softly lit cabin and set her on the floor in front of him.

This time when Daniel kissed her, it was the kiss of a man who wanted a woman.

And Rory responded like a woman who wanted a man. This man.

The kiss started deep and grew deeper. The closer Daniel held her, the closer she wanted to be.

His mouth left hers as he kissed the line of her jaw and warmly nuzzled her ear. Rory tangled her fingers in his hair and tilted her own head back as he kissed her throat. His fingers brushed her damp skin when he unbuttoned her blouse, and his lips followed, moving over the smooth skin of her shoulder and the soft swell of her breast.

Her wet blouse landed on the floor, and then her front-fastening bra.

Daniel's mouth moved between her breasts and over her flat stomach to the top button of her jeans. She felt him tug on the zipper and then lower her wet jeans, following their path with his mouth, over the outside of her thigh. She stepped out of them one leg at a time.

Daniel kissed his way up the inside of her thigh, stopping just short of...

He stood up and stepped back from Rory. His eyes moved lingeringly over her body. "You're beautiful," he said in a hushed voice.

She, normally very modest, wasn't at all embarrassed to be standing in front of him without her clothes. It couldn't have felt more natural. Her eyes moved over his bronze, smooth, muscled body.

Daniel closed his eyes as he pulled her into his arms again and felt her skin warm against his. There had been women in his life. But not one of them had prepared him for what he felt at this moment.

He picked her up and carried her to the bed, then lay beside her. Their lips met again, their legs entwined, and he gently stroked his hand over her back and hips.

Rory explored Daniel with her fingertips, savoring the feel of him. She gently pushed him onto his back and kissed his chest, running her tongue teasingly over his nipple. When her lips brushed over his solid stomach, he caught her under the arms and lifted her on top of him.

"I can't take much of that. Not tonight anyway."

Rory smiled down at him, her face charmingly framed by her damp curls.

He looked into her eyes. "How am I ever going to let you go when the time comes?"

"Maybe it won't."

Daniel rolled her over onto her back, his eyes still on hers. He kissed her long and tenderly, his hand moving over her body, bringing it to pulsing life.

When he entered her, Rory took a sharp breath.

"Are you all right?"

Rory held his face in her hands. "I don't think I've ever been more all right." As Daniel lowered his mouth to hers, she wrapped her legs around him to hold him close. He moved with exquisite slowness, each thrust bringing them closer together.

Something was building inside her. Every time Daniel moved, it grew stronger and stronger. She could feel herself losing control. It was the strangest sensation. There came a point when she knew that no matter what happened, she wouldn't be able to stop.

And then her body just completely let go in the most incredible explosion of feeling imaginable.

Was that her voice she heard?

Daniel raised himself over her. Both of them were out of breath, covered in perspiration.

Rory trembled in what could only be described as an aftershock.

Daniel kissed her over and over again. "Still all right?" he asked. He looked into her teary eyes and pushed her damp hair away from her face.

She nodded.

"What's wrong?"

"Nothing. Nothing at all. I didn't know...." She couldn't find the words.

Daniel lay beside her and pulled her into his arms. "Shh."

She rested her cheek on his shoulder. Her fingers trailed unconsciously over his stomach. She was worried about what he must think of her. "I want you to know that I don't normally jump into bed with men I barely know."

"I didn't think for a moment that you did."

There was something about him, she thought. How could she feel so close to a man she hadn't known until a few days ago?

"I know," he said softly.

She raised her head. "How do you do that?"

"Do what?"

"Read my thoughts. You always seem to know what I'm thinking and feeling without my saying a word."

"I've always known."

"How?"

"One day, when the time is right, you and I will talk."

Rory put her cheek back on his shoulder. "I don't understand any of this."

"You will."

Both of them were tired, but neither wanted to sleep. Rory felt so warm and safe that she just wanted to enjoy it a little longer.

And Daniel felt as though he'd waited all his life to hold Rory in his arms. This might well be their only night together and he wanted to savor it for as long as he could.

Rory couldn't stay awake. The sound of the rain and thunder outside and the warmly crackling fire inside lulled her to sleep.

Daniel heard her soft, even breaths. He moved his lips over her hair. "Oh, Rory," he whispered. "How am I supposed to go on with life as usual when you're gone?

"And you will go."

Chapter Ten

Daniel never went to sleep that night. When morning came, Rory had her back to him and his body was fitted against hers. It felt right.

He loved the smell of her. There was just the barest hint of fragrance, as though it came from her pores and not a bottle.

Rory moved against him and Daniel closed his eyes. He had never wanted a woman the way he wanted her. He had never been aware of another human being the way he was aware of her.

Rory awakened slowly, filled with a sense of inner peace and warmth. She could feel Daniel's body wrapped around hers.

She ran her hand down his strong arm and entwined her fingers with his. He pulled her even closer and kissed the top of her ear.

"I don't want it to be morning," she said softly. She turned around and lay her head on the pillow beside his. "What happens now?"

Daniel touched her cheek with his fingertips. "I'm still Blackhawk. You're still a Milbourne. We go our separate ways."

Rory moved her face closer to his on the pillow and kissed him.

Daniel sighed as he wrapped her in his arms and held her close, then wordlessly climbed out of bed.

Rory's eyes followed him to the bathroom door. A moment later, when she heard the shower, she rolled onto her back and stared at the ceiling.

She refused to regret what had happened last night. But she also knew it couldn't be repeated.

She got out of bed and quickly dressed in her still-damp and crumpled clothes. For the briefest moment, she looked at the bathroom door.

Daniel turned off the shower.

Rory hesitated a moment longer, then slowly walked back to her own cabin to shower and change into clean clothes.

It was going to be a busy day. Finding Bruce and getting some things straight was at the top of her list. Talking to Gray Cloud was next.

She made the assumption that Bruce would use the same motel she had because of its convenience, and that's where she went. There were a couple of rental cars parked in front. No telling which one was his. Instead of trying to guess, she went into the office. The manager greeted her with a smile. "Don't tell me you're coming to stay with us again."

"Not this time. I'm looking for my cousin, Bruce Milbourne."

"He's here. Room 8."

"Thanks."

She found his room not far from where hers had been. Raising her hand, she knocked firmly.

Bruce opened the door a moment later. "I was wondering when you were going to show up."

"I had to find you first. May I come in?"

He opened the door further, then closed it behind her.

"I want to know what you thought you were doing last night."

"Helping you do your job."

"Well, do me a big favor, Bruce, and don't help me any more."

He sat on the bed, all contrition. "I'll concede that I might have been a little out of line last night."

Rory looked at him in amazement. "A little out of line? They were in handcuffs, Bruce."

"That's right. And don't try to tell me they weren't responsible for the sabotage of the equipment."

"I told you last night and I'm telling you now that they wouldn't do that."

"And what if you're wrong?"

"I'm not."

"So we should just eat the damages?"

"I assume the equipment is insured?"

"Of course."

"Then that's exactly what we should do. My guess is that it was one of our men who did it anyway."

"Who?"

"Joe McDermott."

Bruce looked at her as though she'd lost her mind. "Come on, Rory. What would his motive be?"

"To start trouble. That won't be a problem anymore though. I fired him last night."

"You did what?"

"Fired him. On the spot."

"You can't be serious! He was our point man at the site. He knows this operation inside and out."

"He's gone, Bruce, and I won't have him back under any circumstances. I don't like him and I don't trust him. And frankly, at this moment, I'm not real thrilled with you."

"I told you I was just trying to help get things moving. You're wasting time."

"I don't consider getting to know the opposition wasting time. If we can understand what their objections are, we have a chance of being able to change our own strategy so that those objections are eliminated. Everyone gets what they want."

"And if that doesn't work?"

"Then we can talk about getting tough."

Bruce shook his head. "You're too soft for this job. I told my dad he was making a mistake when he sent you here."

"I've got news for you, Bruce. This isn't exactly the high point of my career. If you and your dad want to pull me out of here, I'll be more than happy to go."

He rose from the bed. "Like I said, if it were up to me . . . but it isn't."

Rory turned to open the door. "Go home, Bruce," she said over her shoulder. "I'm going to try to clean up the mess you've made."

Gray Cloud was her next stop. She drove straight back to the reservation and to his house.

After knocking on the door, she waited.

No answer.

She knocked again.

Still no answer.

Rory didn't want to leave without seeing him, so she sat on the porch to wait. This cabin, like the others, was a solitary dwelling. Not lonely, though. She was learning that there was a difference.

She'd been sitting there for quite a while before she became aware of a particular sound that seemed part of the forest—and yet not part of it at all. It sounded something like a flute, but hauntingly different.

Rory got up from the porch and followed the music. It led her to a small clearing in the woods where Gray Cloud sat cross-legged on the ground playing a wooden instrument. She sat on the ground across from him and listened, enraptured.

When he finished his song, he lay the instrument in his lap and looked at Rory in silence.

"That was beautiful," she said. "I've never heard anything quite like that sound before."

"It's a courting flute. This one belonged to my great-grandfather. He taught me to play when I was a child."

Rory sensed that he wasn't finished so she said nothing.

"When the white man came into our lives so long ago, we weren't prepared for the violence or the violation. So many of our people who carried the wisdom of centuries died before they were able to pass it on to the generations that followed. Those of us here now have to go back in time to gather the remaining thread of that wisdom, attempt to unravel it and give it to those who come after." He looked at her. "Do you understand?"

"Yes," she said softly, "I do."

Gray Cloud reached out and covered her hand with his. "You have something to say, child." It was a statement rather than a question.

"I came to apologize for what happened last night."

"It wasn't your doing and it shouldn't be your apology."

"No, but it was my family. I know that neither you nor any of those with you harmed that machinery."

His bright eyes gazed into hers. "How do you know this?"

"No matter how badly you wanted something, you would never behave dishonorably to accomplish it."

He squeezed her hand again and then patted it. "Go now. We'll talk more another day."

Rory wanted to ask him about setting a definite date for a tribal meeting during which she could address the members with her proposal, but she knew that this wasn't the time to push.

As she walked to her car, she reached up to brush her hair away from her face and felt the bandage. She had to get the stitches out. That meant seeing Daniel. She decided to do it now and get it over with.

She drove to the clinic and walked into another full waiting room. Doris smiled up at her as she approached. "Please tell me that you've come to help with more filing."

Rory pointed at her forehead. "Not this time."

"I'll tell Daniel you're here."

"Thank you."

A few minutes later a patient left the examining room. Doris stood in the doorway and beckoned Rory with a bent index finger. Rory walked past her and stopped just a foot into the room. Doris closed the door behind her. Daniel was at the sink washing his hands. He looked up at Rory with a hint of a smile. "I'll be right with you. Take a seat on the table."

Rory sat in the same spot she had when he put the stitches in.

After drying his hands, he picked up a metal tray and set it on the table beside her. "How do you feel?" he asked.

"Fine."

He pushed her hair away from her face. "Hold your hair back," he said.

Rory's hand brushed his as she reached up.

There it was again. That rush of electricity shooting through her. How could she have made it to the age of twenty-five and never had that feeling before?

She watched his face as he leaned over her and did what he had to. She enjoyed looking at him. He had the barest hint of a scar on his chin. She reached up with a gentle hand and touched it. "What happened?"

"I fell out of a tree when I was six."

Rory smiled. "I can imagine you as a child. I bet you got up and went straight back into the tree."

"I did."

Rory was silent for the next few minutes as Daniel finished removing the stitches.

"It looks pretty good," he said when he was done. "It may take a few months for it to blend in with the rest of your skin, but after that I don't think anyone will even notice it."

"Thank you."

Daniel lowered his eyes to hers. He couldn't help cupping her cheek in the palm of his hand and he couldn't prevent the tender expression in his eyes.

Rory's senses went on full alert. "I have to go."

"To do what?"

"Work."

"What kind of work?"

"Putting together a knockout presentation for the people here." Though he didn't move, Rory could feel Daniel's withdrawal.

"You're going to be disappointed by their reaction."

"We'll see."

He stepped away from her. "Can you have it ready by tomorrow?"

Rory hesitated, but just for a moment. "Absolutely."

"Be at tribal headquarters at eight o'clock tomorrow night. I'll make sure there's a good turnout."

Rory looked at him in surprise. "Thank you. But why would you do that for me?"

"Because I already know what the outcome will be and it's time you also knew."

"Ah," she said with a nod. "You think I'll be turned down."

"I do. And what will you do when that happens?"

"I guess we'll just have to take you to court to make sure our rights are protected."

"And the time factor?"

Rory shrugged as she slid off the table. "It will take however long it takes." The words were spoken with more bravado than conviction. She knew her uncle didn't have that kind of time.

Daniel turned away from her as he carried the tray to the sink.

Rory stood there for a moment, wondering if that was his way of dismissing her. She decided it was, and left.

Doris looked up from her work as Rory approached. "Everything go all right?" she asked.

Rory lifted her hair. "All gone, except for the scar."

"That will disappear soon enough."

"I know. How much do I owe you?"

"Nothing. I'm sure Daniel wouldn't think of charging you."

Rory opened her purse, took out a hundred dollars and put it on her desk. "It would have cost at least that much in a regular clinic," she said when Doris would have protested. "Please accept it."

Doris opened a side drawer that held a small cash box. "I'm not one to turn down a gift horse," she said, and put the money inside.

Rory smiled and left. After she climbed into her car, she drove off right away and headed for her cabin. She didn't want to think about Daniel. She couldn't.

As soon as she arrived, she sorted through the pertinent papers, jotted down the necessary figures and carried her working material onto the porch with her so she could work in the sunshine.

She wrote for several hours, creating first one draft and then another, not only doing the number-crunching, but trying as best she could to find a way to phrase what her uncle was proposing in the most favorable way possible.

When she thought she had it laid out the way she wanted it, she jumped into her car, drove to the grocery store and used the outside pay phone she'd noticed at the foot of the driveway.

Calling collect, she went through the usual circuit of people before she finally got her uncle. "Well?" he asked abruptly.

"Good news. Blackhawk is setting up a meeting tomorrow night. I'll be presenting our proposal."

"That's great!"

"I want to read you a draft of what I'm going to say. Stop me wherever you want to make changes."

"Fire away."

Rory started reading. When she finished fifteen minutes later, she waited for her uncle to say something.

"Are you still there?" she finally asked.

"I like it," he said, "but I think we're being just a little too generous with the money. You know as well as I do that, technically, we don't have to pay them a dime."

"I know, but they need to come away from this with something tangible."

"What do you think our chances are?"

Rory sighed. "Not great. The problem is that all we can offer them is the money, and that's not what they're after. They want us to stay off the reservation altogether and leave their hills alone."

"That's not going to happen."

"I know." She felt a sadness she disguised in her voice.

"Call me right after the meeting."

"You know I will."

"Good luck, honey."

Rory hung up and drove back to her little house. It was late afternoon on a beautiful day as she climbed out of her car. She strolled to the lake and sat on the edge. After taking off her shoes, she dangled her feet in the cool water. She had to admit that she was beginning to like the quiet, the isolation. What had at first frightened her, Rory now was beginning to find soothing.

She leaned forward and trailed her fingers through the water.

In her mind's eye, Rory saw Daniel emerging from the water that first morning on the reservation. She looked around to make sure no one was watching. Who would be? She was quite alone.

Standing up, she slipped out of her clothes, folded everything into a neat pile, then waded into the water and swam for a few hundred yards. She had never been swimming without anything on. The feeling of freedom was incredible. Wonderful. She dove and swam underwater, then surfaced and stroked her way back to where she'd started.

As her feet found the bottom, she raised her face from the water and began to wade to shore. An odd noise startled her. It had come from the bank. To her horror, there was a baby bear sniffing around her clothes. "Hey!" she yelled. "Go away. Shoo!"

The cub looked at her, not even a little intimidated, then went back to examining her clothes.

She tried splashing it with water, but she was too far away.

"Shoo!" she yelled again.

This time the bear paid attention—but not before it grabbed her clothes in its mouth and ran into the woods, dragging her jeans and shirt on the ground.

"No, no!" she called after it in frustration. "Come back here with my things!"

Of course it didn't. And there she was, up to her armpits in water and not a stitch in sight.

When she saw Daniel walking toward her, Rory's heart sank. The man must have radar where she was concerned.

He stood on the lake bank and smiled at her. "Problem?" he asked innocently.

"You could say that. A bear just ran off with my clothes."

"Oh," he said with a nod. "That's what all of the yelling was about."

"Don't just stand there. Go after it."

He shook his head. "One thing I learned early in life is that where there's a cub, there's a very protective mother bear nearby."

Rory self-consciously folded her arms across her breasts. "I seem to have a bit of a problem."

Daniel smiled despite himself as he took off his shirt and held it out toward her. "Come on."

"Turn your head away."

"If you'll recall," he say dryly, "I've seen you before."

"That was different." And it was. How could she explain it?

Daniel continued to hold the shirt out, but he did as she asked and turned his head away.

Rory quickly climbed out of the water and slipped her wet arms into his shirt. "You can look now," she said as she bunched the front of it together with her hands.

Daniel turned around, brushed her hands away and buttoned the shirt for her. "You look cold."

"I am," she said with a shiver.

"It gets chilly here at night, even in the summer." He fastened the last button. "Let's go inside. I'll build you a fire."

Rory didn't want to be alone with him. "No," she said quickly, "that's all right. You don't have to do that."

"Of course I don't have to. I want to. Come on."

Rory reluctantly followed him inside. She watched as he lit a match to kindling and logs that had already been laid out by Susan and the others the day before.

"That should help." Daniel straightened away from it and watched the logs slowly catch fire.

"Thank you," she said and she curled up in a chair near the fire. Then she asked the inevitable question. "I don't mean to sound ungrateful for yet another timely rescue, but why are you here?"

Daniel continued to look at the fire. "I spoke with my grandfather about the meeting. He's given his approval. Doris is contacting everyone concerned to tell them about it."

"Thank you," she said. "I really didn't expect this level of cooperation. Particularly after what happened last night."

"My grandfather was reluctant to have the meeting this soon. He wanted you to spend more time here getting to know us and what it is you're asking us to sacrifice. I convinced him that your staying longer would change nothing. You're here for your uncle, and neither weeks nor months will change the focus of your loyalty."

Rory didn't say anything.

"This way you'll have your answer and will be able to move on. We both will." His eyes rested on her for a long moment before he walked past her to the door.

"Will you be there tomorrow night?" she asked.

"Yes."

And then he was gone.

Rory uncurled herself from her chair, went to the door, still in Daniel's shirt, and watched him walk away. If all went well tomorrow, she'd be leaving here. Even if it didn't, she supposed she'd still be leaving.

She couldn't imagine never seeing him again.

A man she'd known less than a week.

Turning back to her cabin, Rory closed the door. It was only around eight-thirty and just getting dark, but she was tired. And perhaps a little depressed. She lay down on the bed in Daniel's shirt, fully intending to get up in a few minutes.

She didn't. The warmth of the fire, softness of the bed and the scent of Daniel that clung to his shirt lulled her into a sound and dreamless sleep that lasted until morning.

Chapter Eleven

Rory showed up at tribal headquarters at exactly eight o'clock. There were so many people there that the cars spilled out of the parking lot and onto the sides of the roads. Rory parked what was perhaps the city equivalent of a block away, lifted her file from the passenger seat and walked to the headquarters.

Like so many of the other buildings, this one was made from logs, but it was big. Certainly large enough for several hundred people.

This was it.

Rory wished herself good luck and opened the door.

The conversational hum that filled the meeting room was instantly hushed. As Rory walked through the people, some smiled at her and some didn't. She spotted Susan, Jake and Little Jake and quietly waved at them. Gray Cloud was already seated in the front row. Daniel was with him, but standing.

As soon as he saw her, he took her by the arm to a podium at the front of the hall.

"Be seated, everyone," he said into the attached microphone.

There was a lot of rustling while people found their places.

"You all know why we're here," he said. "This is Ms. Rory Milbourne. She's here as the attorney for her uncle's corporation. Listen carefully to what she has to say. When she's finished, we'll have open discussion and then take a vote." He stepped away from the podium and stood off to the side.

Rory opened her file and smiled at the people. "Hello."

The microphone was too high, so she adjusted it. "As Mr. Blackhawk already told you, I'm here to represent Milbourne Corporation. A few months ago, we acquired the government's permission to mine for copper in your hills. Since the reservation is technically governmental land, we've been operating under the assumption that our dealings had nothing to do with those of you who live here. We've now seen how important the hills are to you and have come to the conclusion that for us to not include you from the very beginning was a mistake."

She looked at the faces to see how she was going over.

It didn't look like good news.

Rory didn't give up, though. She dug back in and spoke to them the way she would speak to friends, putting forth her honest appraisal of what was in the hills and how much of it the tribe would receive if they gave their permission to mine them.

On a tougher note, she told them that if it was necessary to take them to court, her company would win because the law was on their side, and the tribe would end up with nothing.

Her entire presentation took less than half an hour. She mapped everything out in detail, including things the money could be used for.

There was absolutely no feedback. No one had any questions or comments. Even as she closed her file and stepped away from the podium, she, who was usually very good at reading people, had no idea where she stood.

Daniel walked over to her, took her arm and led her through the people. "You go back to your cabin," he said. "We'll discuss things, take a vote, and I'll let you know what happens."

"You'll tell me as soon as you know?"

"That's right."

"What if they have questions?"

"You told us all you need to."

That was it. There was nothing more she could do.

She turned to leave. Daniel closed the door behind her.

Rory drove to her little cabin and sat on the porch to wait. She saw the wolf silently approaching and didn't feel the least bit of fear as he went past her onto the porch and lay down about five feet away.

"I think I know how this is going to end," she said quietly to her companion. "I don't know what I'm going to tell my uncle."

The wolf quietly eyed her.

"I promised him I wouldn't let him down."

It was eleven o'clock when she saw Daniel walking toward her in the moonlight.

She rose and waited for the news.

Daniel stopped in front of her. "They voted no," he said.

Her heart sank. "By what percentage?"

"Seventy-five."

Rory sat down on the step.

"Are you all right?"

"No. Everything my uncle has was riding on being able to mine in the hills."

Daniel's dark eyes softened. "I won't say I'm sorry that we turned your offer down, but I am sorry about the situation your uncle finds himself in."

Her keys were in her pocket. She rose again, walked past Daniel to her car. "I have to tell him. He's waiting for my call."

Daniel watched as she drove off. He'd wanted to take her in his arms, but knew her well enough not to. This was a very serious business. He thought about waiting for her to return, but decided against that, as well, and went to his own house.

Rory drove slowly to the grocery store and parked near the phone. She sat in her car for several minutes, trying to think what to tell him to ease the blow, but there was really no way to sugarcoat the truth.

It was with a heavy heart that she called his house collect. He answered on the first ring, as though he'd been waiting. When the operator finally got off the line, her uncle couldn't get the words out fast enough. "Tell me what happened."

"We were voted down."

"Damn!"

"I'm sorry."

"What happened?"

"They took their hills over our money."

"Any chance of our changing their minds?"

"I'd have to say no. Only twenty-five percent of the people voted in our favor."

"So that's it," he said sadly.

"I'm afraid so. I'll come back tomorrow and get the court papers ready for filing."

"We've been through this, Rory. There's no time."

"It's all we can do."

There was silence at the other end of the line.

"Uncle Bill?"

"I have to go, Rory. I can't talk about this right now."

"Are you all right?"

"No. I'm in one hell of a situation."

"I know. I'm so sorry."

"It's not your fault. This project has been cursed from the beginning. I wish I'd never gotten myself involved."

"I'll see you tomorrow."

"Yeah. Good night, Rory." He sounded so defeated. It broke her heart. Before she could say anything else, he hung up.

Rory climbed back into her car. She didn't know she was crying until the tears spilled down her cheeks. She impatiently dashed them away with the back of her hand and went back to her cabin.

Daniel was gone.

The wolf was gone.

She went inside the cabin and packed most of her things, then went outside to sit on the porch.

Her emotions were in a strange tug-of-war. On the one hand, she was devastated at how things had turned out for her uncle. On the other hand, in only a few days she'd come to the conclusion that the mining would have been disastrous for the tribe. She was nearly as relieved as she was upset. She was going to have to go back to Chicago and make an all-out effort to help her uncle fix the mess he was in.

And perhaps there was a little part of her that wondered if she couldn't have done more.

She sat there for a long time, thinking about everything and nothing.

And then she noticed something odd in the air. A strange smell. Acrid.

She took a deep breath. Smoke. Sitting up straight, she looked around and saw a red glow coming from the direction of Daniel's cabin. Rory took off like a shot down the path and reached the end only to see the entire structure engulfed in flame.

"Daniel!" She screamed his name as she ran around the house.

When she finally saw him, standing completely still, perspiration glistening on his damp skin and glowing in the light of the fire, all she could think was that he was alive. She put her arms around Daniel and held him.

Daniel embraced her, as well, but his eyes were on his home.

Jake brought his car to a skidding stop just a few feet away from them. "Daniel," he called out the window, "we've got fires all over the reservation."

Daniel's face hardened. "My grandfather?" he asked.

"His home is gone, but he's with Susan. He's fine."

"The clinic?"

"I'm sorry, Daniel. It's completely gone."

Daniel dropped his arm from Rory's shoulders. His angry dark eyes reflected the flames. "You did this "

It took Rory a moment to understand what he was saying, it was so unexpected. Her eyes reflected her shock. "You can't possibly believe that!"

"What I believe is that your uncle is capable of doing anything to get what he wants. He set the fires before as a warning, and he set these to intimidate us."

"You're wrong. You couldn't be more wrong. He isn't that kind of man." She looked pleadingly at Jake. "Tell him that we had nothing to do with this."

"I'm sorry, Rory," he said with genuine sadness, "but these fires are deliberate, and there's no one else with a motive."

"I'm going with Jake," said Daniel, "and I want you off this reservation by daylight."

"No."

That wasn't the answer Daniel was expecting. "What?"

"I said no." She opened the rear door of Jake's car, climbed inside and closed it. "There has to be something I can do to help and that's exactly what I'm going to do. And if you don't like it, Daniel, tough."

Despite the seriousness of the situation, Jake smiled. No one ever talked to Daniel like that. It was good for him.

Daniel certainly wasn't smiling when he silently climbed into the passenger seat and closed the door with a little more force than was absolutely necessary.

Jake took off with a spin of his tires and drove straight to the tribal headquarters. There were a lot of people wandering around, some crying. Rory got out of the car, spotted Susan and went to her. "What can I do?"

Susan smiled and touched her arm. "Help get the children settled inside. Most of their parents stayed at their homes to either fight fires that had already been set, or guard their property against any new threat. Some others are in the main kitchen making coffee and sandwiches. You can help there, as well."

As Rory turned to go into the building, she saw Jake and Daniel driving away. But there was no time to worry. She was swept into a sea of activity. Both young women and old were laying out sleeping bags, blankets and pillows on the floor to accommodate the children. Rory grabbed some blankets from a table and began to help. She was aware of the suspicious way the women were looking at her, but she helped anyway.

When the last blanket had been used, Rory helped settle the children down and tuck them in. Some of them were crying, and their mothers lay beside them, singing softly or talking in a soothing whisper.

Rory spent extra time with those children who were on their own, making sure they felt safe and comfortable.

When things in the main room were pretty quiet, she went into the large kitchen to see what she could do there. Again, she was met with suspicious looks, but no real hostility. There were perhaps a dozen people there, but only one who appeared to be in charge. Rory approached her. "I'm here to help. What can I do?"

The woman looked for a moment as though she were going to tell her to leave but thought better of it. "We could use some extra hands to make sandwiches. Bread, meat and cheese are on that table," she said as she pointed. There was another woman already working there.

"And if you're willing, we could use your help in getting some of this food delivered to where it's needed."

"I am. Tell me where and when."

"Thank you."

Rory walked over to the table and stood next to the woman who was working there. "I was asked to help you."

It was the woman from the grocery store. She looked at Rory without smiling and pushed a loaf of bread toward her.

Rory worked quickly, stacking the sandwiches one on top of the other, then slicing through all of them with a knife before setting them on a tray. When it was full, she covered it with plastic wrap and started on the next one. As she was wrapping that one, Susan walked over to Rory and tapped her on the shoulder. "You and I are going to deliver some of this now."

"I can do it on my own," said Rory. "You're needed here."

"You don't know where to go."

"Let me guess," said Rory. "You're the only one they could find who's willing to go with me."

"I'm afraid so."

"All right. What car are we using?"

"It's the black truck parked right in front of the door."

"I'll carry these out and meet you there."

Rory did a balancing act to get through the people and out the door. As she put the trays into the back of the truck, Susan and two other women came with coolers filled with ice, water, soda and anything else anyone had, and hoisted them into the back. Susan climbed in behind the wheel, Rory got into the passenger seat and off they went.

Rory realized within a mile that Susan was right about not being able to find her way. There seemed to be an endless number of fires, if the red glows Rory saw were any indication.

And then Rory saw a huge glow in the distance. That was no house. It looked as though the entire forest were burning.

Rory moved closer to the edge of her seat. "My, God," she breathed.

Susan stopped the car in the middle of the road and looked. "It's moving fast."

"Tell me that's not where Daniel and Jake are."

"That's exactly where they are, along with dozens of others."

"We have to get there."

Susan put the truck into gear and sped toward the fire. It took them nearly half an hour to reach the site where most of the men had parked. Susan pulled her little truck among them. Both women hopped out. Rory grabbed the sandwich trays while Susan lifted a manageable cooler of ice water and cups, and set out in search of the men. They found them perhaps a five-minute walk away, digging trenches, removing undergrowth and trying to create a firebreak to keep the flames from spreading.

Both Susan and Rory looked anxiously around for Jake and Daniel as the men and women briefly left their work to grab some food and drink.

Susan was the one who asked the question of one of the exhausted men. "Where are the others?"

"They're closer to the fire," he said between mouthfuls. "We're trying to create a wide break. They're at the other end working their way toward us."

"We have to go there," said Susan.

"No," said Rory, shaking her head as she lifted one of the trays and picked up a still-full cooler. "You stay here. I'll go."

"But..."

"Look, you have a child to worry about. I don't. Let me at least do this."

Susan hesitated but knew Rory was right. If something terrible happened, Little Jake would need her.

She watched with dread as Rory disappeared into the forest.

Rory had no idea where she was or where she was going. The only thing she did was walk straight and hope to run into them.

Her arms were going to break. Rory stopped for a moment and set the tray and cooler on the ground while she shook her aching arms to restore circulation. Just a minute later, she picked them back up and started walking.

It was with relief that she heard the sound of raised voices and people working. When she finally arrived at the site, the men and two or three women with them stopped what they were doing and surrounded her as they made a quick grab for food and drink and immediately went back to work.

Jake took a sandwich and winked at her. Daniel, his face covered with soot, took something to drink but didn't look at her at all.

She couldn't just stand there while the others worked. She set everything down, grabbed an ax and started chopping away with the rest of them.

Daniel raised his head and looked at her in complete disapproval, but said nothing.

Rory chopped until she thought her arms were going to fall off. The heat from the fire approaching behind them was like a blanket of uncomfortable warmth on an otherwise cool night. She could hear the crackle of burning trees and the pop of sap brought to the boiling point.

It was getting too close. "That's it!" yelled Daniel. "Let's get out of here."

Rory went after the tray and cooler.

Daniel grabbed them from her. "Go on," he said impatiently. "There's no time to lose."

She ran ahead of him all the way to the other side of the firebreak. As soon as Daniel made sure everyone was clear, he and several other men lit torches and set fire to the brush and trees inside the firebreak.

Everyone stood back and watched as the fire caught, accelerated and grew huge. Because of the large dirt trench that had been dug, the fire burned away from them and toward the other fire.

Minutes ticked by. They all just watched. Susan and Jake stood with their arms around each other. Rory stood off by herself.

Ten, fifteen, thirty minutes ticked by. And then the two fires met head-on—and died. There was no fuel left to feed the flames.

There was a lot of backslapping and high-fives.

Except by Daniel, Rory noticed. He stood quietly, staring at the smoldering remains of what had been part of a beautiful forest. Then he walked to Susan. "How's my grandfather?"

"I don't know, Daniel. He left the headquarters not long after he arrived. He seemed fine."

Daniel nodded. "He probably went home. Or at least to what's left of it." He looked at Rory and pointed at her. "I'm taking you back to the cabin. I want you to pack your things and go."

"I told you that my uncle didn't do this. He's morally incapable of causing this kind of destruction."

"Who are you trying to convince, Rory, me or yourself?"

She had no response.

He turned to Jake. "You go with Susan and I'll take your truck. I'll get it back to you tonight."

Jake tossed him the keys.

Susan, braving Daniel's disapproval, walked up to Rory and hugged her tightly. "I'm going to miss you. Keep in touch."

Rory was close to tears. "Bye," she whispered.

Daniel started walking. Rory took one last look at Susan and Jake and fell into step behind him. They climbed into the truck in silence and made the long drive to Gray Cloud's without saying a word. As Daniel shoved the gear into Park, he sat there for a moment with his hands on the steering wheel. "I want to make sure my grandfather's all right," he said without looking at her. "You stay in the truck."

"All right," she said quietly.

He sat there for a moment longer and then climbed out.

Rory leaned her head back against the seat. Clouds came and went, at times obscuring the moon and making it difficult to see. But when they did clear, she saw what was left of Gray Cloud's cabin.

It was gone.

Smoke still rose from the flattened ruins. Rory pressed her fingertips to her lips and this time didn't try to stop the tears from falling. It was horrible.

Rory felt like the sides of the truck were closing in on her. She clumsily reached for the hand crank to roll down the window and then leaned her face outside to breathe in the cool air.

That's when she heard it, the soft, melodic chanting. She knew it was Gray Cloud.

Daniel could see his grandfather in the moonlight. He was sitting cross-legged on the ground, facing the lake, his eyes closed, chanting. He stood quietly behind him and watched, waited.

After a few minutes, his grandfather stopped and opened his eyes. "You're blaming the wrong person, Daniel," he said, not turning to look at him. "This isn't your Rory's doing."

"It's her family."

"You can't hold her responsible for what someone in her family has done."

"I can and I do. We're lucky no one was killed tonight." He dragged his fingers through his hair. "We still don't know how many homes were destroyed. And the clinic we struggled so hard to put together is nothing more than dust."

"All of this can be rebuilt."

"She's leaving tonight."

"You love her."

"It doesn't matter."

Gray Cloud turned to look at his cherished grandson. He knew that Rory was already carrying Daniel's child. "When she leaves, she won't be leaving alone."

Daniel frowned at his grandfather. "I don't know what you mean."

"If you send her away now, you could lose her forever."

"I have a responsibility to my people. You taught me that from the time I was a child. I can't look at the destruction this woman's family has wrought and allow myself to love her. Surely you understand that, Grandfather."

"All too well. But when it comes to Rory, it isn't a matter of allowing yourself to love her. You do. You always have and you always will. No one will ever be able to replace her in your heart. You'll carry around an emptiness for the rest of your days."

"Then that's the way it will have to be."

Gray Cloud went back to staring at the lake.

"I have her waiting in the truck. I stopped here because I needed to make sure you were all right."

"I will be."

"You can sleep at the tribal headquarters tonight. We can work out something more permanent tomorrow."

"I'm going to stay here, Daniel."

"It's cold."

"I like the cold. You go do what you have to and don't worry about me. I prefer being alone."

Daniel hated to leave him there, but he deferred to his grandfather's wishes and went back to the truck. He said nothing as he climbed in and started the engine.

Rory wanted to ask him if Gray Cloud was all right but couldn't find her voice. She sat in silence for the ride to her cabin—still standing untouched by the selective disaster.

Daniel stopped in front of it. Rory didn't get out right away. She just couldn't leave like this. How many ways could she tell him her uncle wasn't responsible?

As had happened so often before, Daniel read her thoughts. He turned his head to look at her. "If I were you," he said, "I'd check things out before declaring Milbourne Corporation innocent."

Rory opened the door and stepped out. As soon as she closed it, Daniel drove away.

What she didn't see was him pulling to the side of the road a mile away, sitting there with the engine idling, gripping the steering wheel so hard his knuckles were white, his expression grieved as though someone he loved had died.

Rory allowed herself the luxury of feeling good and sorry for herself for all of five minutes. Then she pulled herself back together, walked into the cabin, threw her remaining unpacked clothes and files into her suitcase and, without bothering to check to see if she'd left anything behind, she loaded her car and started driving. She was going straight back to Chicago to do exactly as Daniel had suggested and mount her own investigation of the history of this mining deal.

From there she would track every letter, phone call, legal paper, treaty—anything that might have something to do with what had happened on Whispering Pines that night. And when she had all of her facts together, she'd bring them to Daniel and show him how wrong he was. She had to admit that the timing of the fires was suspicious, but there had been fires before the vote was taken and no one knew the source.

And while she was doing that, she would see about getting some financial aid to those who had lost their homes and to rebuild the clinic for Daniel.

Even if the rift between them was so great it could never be mended, she had to do that.

It was midmorning when she arrived at the airport. There weren't any flights to Chicago until the evening, so she waited. And waited.

Her thoughts raced around madly without taking on any particular direction.

She was exhausted.

When her plane finally arrived at the gate, she boarded and took a window seat. It was a short flight—less than an hour.

She was asleep before they left the ground.

Chapter Twelve

An hour was enough. As soon as the plane touched down in Chicago, Rory got her luggage, found her car in the lot, paid the fee and headed for the office.

When she arrived at the underground parking garage, it was nearly eight o'clock in the evening. She found the office deserted, as she'd expected.

She flipped on the lights in Mary's office and then in her own, dropped onto her desk the file she'd taken with her and the one Mary had mailed, and went into Mary's office in search of more files. She pulled out anything that had a mention of copper mines and Whispering Pines, lugged them back to her office and sat at her desk to begin the task of sorting through the voluminous material.

With papers in her hand, she read while absent-mindedly starting a pot of strong coffee. She poured herself a mugful and drank as she paced in her office.

Hours and a sizable stack of already-read papers later, she hadn't found anything that wasn't absolutely aboveboard in either the corporation's dealings with the government, the mining company or with the reservation itself.

But she kept going. She wouldn't be satisfied until she'd read every scrap of paper.

She found an interesting reference to Joe McDermott. Apparently he wasn't originally with the mining company they'd hired, but had been brought in by her uncle to head up the crew.

That wasn't particularly unusual, but it bothered her. Her uncle usually had good instincts about people. If he'd hired Joe himself, surely he would have seen what kind of man he was.

She kept digging.

There were several references to a particular congressman. She knew he'd assisted her uncle and Bruce in getting the initial geologic surveys done on the reservation. Again, there was nothing particularly unusual in that contact.

When she'd gone through every piece of paper in the files, Rory sat back in her chair and stared at the far wall of her office. She just wasn't satisfied that she'd seen everything. Joe McDermott and the congressman were loose ends that didn't come together in any of the documentation she'd read.

So perhaps there were other files.

Determined to satisfy herself, she went into her cousin's office first. He had no locked drawers or filing cabinets, so Rory went through everything.

There was nothing there.

She went into her uncle's office, sat behind his desk and tried to open his bottom desk drawer.

It was locked.

Feeling a little like a thief, she took a letter opener from the top of the desk and used it to pry the drawer open. To her surprise, it worked. She pulled it open and, with some dread, looked inside. There were three files, none of them labeled.

She pulled the top one out and opened it. The first thing she saw was a handwritten record of a payment of $25,000 in cash to Joe McDermott.

Rory's heart sank to her toes. Since when did anyone get that kind of money for just showing up at work? And in cash, no less.

She worked her way through the files page by page. There was a record of several payments made to the same congressman mentioned in the other files. The first one was almost two years earlier.

There were documents that explored having the tribe evicted from the reservation altogether by using some obscure ruling by a Wisconsin court in the early 1800s, and correspondence between her uncle and a Wisconsin attorney that discussed eviction as a viable option in order to get at the copper.

The final nail in her uncle's coffin, as far as Rory was concerned, was a hand-penned memo he had written to himself the day before that outlined what he

intended to do if the tribe voted against the mining.
There was nothing in it about fire, but referred to
"regrettably drastic measures" that needed to be taken
immediately to "further the cause" and "allow freedom of movement" on the reservation. And there was
the added notation that Joe McDermott had been paid
an additional $25,000 without any explanation about
what the money was for.

Rory stared blindly at the paper in front of her.

Her uncle had done it. He'd been so desperate to
save his own financial skin that he'd destroyed the lives
of the people on Whispering Pines Reservation without so much as a regretful thought.

Daniel was right.

She sat behind the desk, unmoving, as the sun rose
outside and shone red through the tinted office windows, and she waited.

She heard Mary arrive.

She heard Bruce arrive.

And finally her uncle's voice came to her as he
cheerfully greeted Mary.

"You're certainly in a better mood than you have
been for a while," said the secretary.

"It's a beautiful morning, Mary. And I'm expecting good news."

"I'll keep my fingers crossed for you," Mary re-
plied.

"Has Rory called?"

"No."

"As soon as she does, interrupt whatever I'm doing. I need to speak with her."

"Of course."

He saw Rory as soon as he opened his office door. His smile was replaced by a look of complete surprise. "Rory! What are you doing here?"

"I need to talk to you."

He closed the door behind him. "So talk."

"There were fires on the reservation the night before last."

She was amazed at how sincerely distressed he appeared to be. "I know. I hope no one was hurt."

"Not physically, but a lot of people lost their homes along with all their possessions. Daniel Blackhawk's clinic, the only one on the entire reservation, burned to the ground."

"Well, as hard-pressed as I am to sympathize with anything bad happening to that thorn in my side, I wouldn't wish this kind of bad luck on anyone."

"I don't think the fires had anything to do with luck, Uncle Bill, bad or otherwise."

For the first time, Bill Milbourne noticed the file that was open in front of Rory. "What are you doing with my private papers?"

A corner of her mouth lifted, but there was no amusement. "Oddly enough," she said as she rose, "I was attempting to prove to Daniel and everyone else on the reservation that you had nothing to do with the fires. Silly me."

Her uncle moved around the desk and closed the file. "You're misinterpreting what you saw."

"No, I'm not. You didn't set the fires yourself, of course, but you hired Joe McDermott to do it for you. I'm sure he's the one who set the earlier fires, too."

"You don't know what you're talking about."

"I certainly didn't until a few hours ago."

"Rory, I swear to you..."

"Oh, stop it," she said angrily. "We both know what happened. What I want to know is why? Why would you do something like that to those people? What have they ever done to harm you? What have they ever done to deserve what you did to them?"

Bill looked at his niece for a long time before speaking. She looked exhausted and her face was smudged with soot. "They wouldn't listen to reason," he said simply. "Sending you there was my last rational option. When they turned down our offer with such a resounding majority, I knew that no amount of lobbying them in an effort to earn their goodwill would work. All I could hope to do was scare them off the land. Or, at least, frighten the ones who voted against the mining into changing their votes. I told you before you went there how desperately I need this deal."

"Yes," she said quietly, "you did. But never for a moment did I think that you would resort to something like this. It's beyond my comprehension."

"I did what had to be done." He shoved the file away from him as though that would get rid of the problem. "You can consider yourself removed from this matter. Bruce will take it from here. And he'll get the votes we need for the mining."

"You're 'removing' me from this matter?" asked Rory. "Oh, no. I don't think so. As of this moment I'm your ex-employee."

"Are you going to the authorities?" he asked.

"I'm going back to Whispering Pines to tell them exactly what you've been doing. If they want to file charges against you, that's up to them. I personally hope they do."

"How can you do this to me? How can you choose them over me?" he asked.

Rory's throat constricted. It was a moment before she could answer. "Uncle Bill, you took me into your home when you certainly didn't have to. You gave me love and support. You're as close to me as a father. But no matter how I feel about you, I could never condone the terrible thing you've done. And I can't let you get away with it."

"If you tell anyone about this, I'll be ruined. Not just financially, but my reputation."

"I know."

"Rory," he pleaded, "you can't do this to me."

"You've done it to yourself." The words were spoken with a quiet sadness.

"I'll never forgive you."

"I know." She picked the files up off his desk and turned to leave.

"These people are nobody," he said angrily. "So a few homes burned. We're not talking about mansions and priceless art. No one was hurt."

Rory didn't even bother to respond as she walked out the door and closed it behind her.

Mary looked up in surprise. "What are you doing here? I thought you were still in Wisconsin."

"I got here last night. I'd appreciate it if you'd arrange for someone to pack up the personal items in my office and messenger them to my apartment. I won't be coming back here."

Mary rose from behind her desk. "What are you talking about?"

"I'm leaving."

"But..."

Rory hugged her. "Don't ask me any questions."

She went to the parking garage and climbed into her car. Her hand was poised over the ignition, but it fell to her lap as blinding tears spilled onto her cheeks. She could talk big about it being her uncle's own fault, but the fact was that she was responsible for whatever was going to happen to him from this moment forward.

She was responsible for his ruin.

Rory pulled herself together and drove to her apartment. When she walked in the door, she tossed her keys onto the hall table and went straight to her bathroom.

The woman who looked back at her was a stranger. Her face was smudged from the fire two nights ago. Under her eyes there were circles so dark she looked as though she were injured. Her clothes were dirty. No wonder the other passengers on the plane had looked at her so strangely.

Rory stripped out of her clothes, turned on her shower and stepped under the steamy spray. For a long time she just stood there and let the water run over her.

It was all she could do to work up the energy to scrub herself and wash her hair, but she did.

When she was finished, she wrapped herself in a big terry-cloth robe and sank onto the edge of her bed. Picking up the phone, she pressed the number for information in the Whispering Pines Reservation area code and asked for Jake Troyat's home phone.

Then she hung up and stared at the phone for a full minute before picking up the receiver and punching in the number with renewed determination. Susan answered.

"It's me," said Rory.

"Hello! Did you get home all right?"

"Yes." She tried to make her voice sound normal, but it was husky from exhaustion and stress. "I'd like you to give Jake a message for me."

"Of course."

"Tell him that I have some information about the fires and some other incidents. I'll be bringing it to him tomorrow."

"Do you want him to call you?"

"No, that's not necessary. I'm going to drive rather than fly. If I leave here early in the morning, I should be there around three or four in the afternoon."

Susan paused. "Do you want to see Daniel while you're here?"

"I'd rather not, but I suppose that's the coward's way out. I can speak with him at the same time I meet with Jake."

"I'll tell him to expect you."

"Thanks, Susan. And tell Jake that he should watch out for Joe McDermott."

"Did he set the fires?"

"I think so."

"Rory, maybe you should—"

"I don't want to talk anymore right now. Just give Jake the message and I'll see both of you tomorrow."

"I understand.

"Bye."

After Rory hung up, she sat there a minute longer then lay back on her bed. She was completely exhausted.

Within seconds, she was asleep.

Chapter Thirteen

Just before turning onto the dirt road that ran through the reservation, Rory pulled her car over to the side and sat there. Her courage nearly failed her.

Nearly, but not quite.

She put the car back into gear and made the turn.

As much as she was dreading what was to come, she still felt a comfortable familiarity as she drove down the dirt road. It seemed strangely as though she were coming home.

She drove slowly, putting off the inevitable, looking from one side of the road to the other to see if any of the fire damage was visible.

It wasn't.

She was well into the reservation when she came across a truck blocking the road. Rory put her car into Park and got out to see if it was some kind of accident, or to see if there was some way to move the truck so she could get by.

She walked all around it. There didn't seem to be any damage to the truck, and no one was inside.

With her hands on her hips, she tried to figure a way around it, but the road on either side was too narrow for passing.

Someone suddenly came up behind her, put her in a headlock and began dragging her backward into the woods. Rory was so shocked she couldn't even scream at first, but struggled with all of her strength against the person dragging her.

Her mind shut down. Rory was running on instinct, and her instincts were good. As soon as she saw an opening, she took it and sank her teeth into a meaty arm.

The man swore and loosened his grip enough for Rory to wiggle free and start running.

She didn't get far, though. The man tackled her, slamming her to the ground with such force that he knocked the wind out of her. She panicked when she couldn't draw any air into her lungs, sure that she was going to die.

The man took his knee out of the middle of her back and flipped her over.

It was Joe McDermott.

She kept trying to get air, all the while her eyes on the man towering over her.

"What are you doing?" she was finally able to ask.

"You think I don't know why you're here?"

Rory didn't answer.

"You're not going to drag me into this, lady. No way."

"I'm not dragging you into anything, McDermott. You're the one who set the fires, and you're going to have to pay the price along with my uncle."

"No one can prove I set anything."

"Maybe not, but I'm sure your bank balance can point investigators in the right direction."

"You little..." He leaned over her and raised his arm as though he were going to backhand her. She readied herself for the blow, but it never came. He dropped his hand. "Let me tell you my scenario," he said.

Rory waited.

"You're going to disappear. It will be as though you never existed. Everyone will blame the Indians. After all, you're not exactly a popular figure here these days. And this is where you were headed when you disappeared. I can see the headlines now. And I can see a shift in sympathy. In fact, if there's a big enough uproar, we may just get to mine that copper after all."

"You're crazy."

He shook his head. "No. Just one up on you."

Rory started to rise from the ground, but he shoved her back down with his foot on her shoulder. "You lay there until I tell you to get up. Understand?"

Rory didn't say anything.

He roughly shoved her again. "Understand?"

"Yes," she said tightly.

He looked around to make sure they were alone. "Sit up."

She did.

"Put your hands behind your back."

"Oh, come on."

"Do it!"

With a sigh of exasperation that masked her growing fear, she did as he ordered. He took some rope out of his pocket and bound her wrists and ankles. "There," he said, when he was finished and straightened away from her. "That should hold you for a few minutes. Don't try anything and maybe I won't hurt you when I get back."

Rory looked at him in disbelief. "You just, in effect, told me you were going to kill me."

He shook his head, all innocence. "I didn't use that word."

"How else am I going to 'disappear'?"

"Your imagination is far too vivid," he said, and walked away from her. "And I meant what I said about not trying anything. I'll only be gone a few minutes."

She stayed perfectly still with only her mind racing, until he was out of sight. Hopping was out. Scooting would get her nowhere fast. Rolling seemed to make the most sense.

And that's exactly what she did. Stretching her full length on the ground, she started moving one revolution at a time, making necessary adjustments to avoid coming into contact with trees.

She made it perhaps a hundred yards from where McDermott had left her. There was an old and very thick-trunked tree. She managed to rise to her feet and hide behind it.

And she waited.

And waited.

Rory strained her ears listening for some noise—something—anything that would tell her what was going on. She didn't dare peek around the trunk of the tree for fear of being seen.

She heard a car start. The engine noise faded as though the car were leaving. It sounded like her car.

A frown creased her forehead. Had the man just been playing a game with her? Was he going to leave her like this rather than come back to finish the job he'd started?

Still, she wouldn't look. Just in case.

She heard another car start. His? she wondered. That sound also faded.

More waiting.

She heard his footsteps first, crunching through the leaves and pine needles. Then she heard him swear sharply, no doubt when he realized she was gone.

Her heart flew into her throat.

"You might as well come out," he said, his voice drawing nearer. "I'll find you eventually. Save us both some time."

Rory looked hurriedly around for a weapon. She saw a pretty sturdy stick, and tried to figure out how to use it effectively with bound hands.

She couldn't. She couldn't even pick it up off the ground without making her presence known.

His footsteps grew closer.

Rory held her breath. Even her heartbeat seemed suspended.

And then he was there, angrily looking at her. "I told you not to move."

Rory didn't bother trying to hide her animosity. "Why would you think that I'd do anything you told me to?"

This time he did hit her.

Rory refused to cower. If anything, she stood straighter and her eyes stared directly into his.

"Stop looking at me like that," he ordered.

When she didn't, he slapped her again. Then he grabbed Rory and slung her over his shoulder in a fireman's carry.

By the time he stopped walking twenty minutes later, Rory had no idea where she was. He roughly unloaded her onto the ground and looked around as he tried to figure out what he was going to do with her.

Rory watched him in silence, more wary than afraid, trying, like a chess player, to figure out what his next move was going to be and how she was going to counter it.

He sat down about ten feet away from Rory and stared at her in silence.

"How did you know I was coming?" she asked.

"Your uncle called me."

"Did he tell you to do this?"

"No. He just wanted me to take off."

She found some comfort in that. "Why didn't you?"

"Because I think this is a better solution. You're the one who's causing the problem. I get rid of you and there's no problem."

"Not if you're willing to up the charges against you from arson to murder."

"No one knows I'm here."

"I think the authorities will be able to figure it out."

"And no one knows you're here."

"Yes, they do."

He shook his head. "They know you were headed here, but who's to say you ever arrived?"

"My car is here."

"It'll be at the bottom of the lake with you in it."

Rory looked at him for a long moment. "I can see that you've given this a lot of thought."

"That's right."

"So why are we here? Why aren't I already in the lake?"

His eyes moved over her body in a way that made the hair on the back of her neck stand on end. "I'm not sure I'm finished with you just yet, Ms. Milbourne."

All of her senses went on full alert as he rose from the ground and walked toward her.

"Don't do this." She asked but didn't plead.

"Who's going to stop me?"

"Please."

"You're not so tough now, are you?" He leaned over and grasped her face in a bruising grip. "No. Not so tough. How does it feel to be on the receiving end instead of dishing it out?''

Rory said nothing as she looked straight into his eyes.

He raised his hand as if to strike her. Rory stiffened and waited for the blow.

Suddenly, out of the forest, one of the most frightening growls she'd ever heard erupted. Before the man could react, the wolf came flying through the air and clamped his teeth on McDermott's raised arm.

The big man fell onto the ground with a loud scream. He did everything he possibly could to get the wolf off him, but the animal refused to let go.

Rory watched in fascinated horror as McDermott managed to kick the wolf. This time the animal did let go with a yelp. As McDermott got to his feet and started running, the wolf chased him down and buried his teeth in his leg.

There was another ferocious wrestling match between man and wolf, and the wolf was winning.

This time when the wolf let go, it was clearly his own idea. McDermott took off running again. The wolf didn't chase him, but stood in perfect stillness and watched.

After several minutes, the wolf trotted back to Rory and sat beside her, alert and protective.

She couldn't believe it. ''Oh,'' she said, and struggled with the ropes around her wrists, ''if I could get these things off, I'd give you the scratching of a lifetime.''

The wolf looked at her with his remarkable golden eyes.

"Or not," she said. "You don't really strike me as the scratching type."

It was obvious that she wasn't going to be able to work the ropes loose. She looked around for something sharp or rough she could use to cut through the cords. Tree bark was the best she could come up with.

She scooted herself to a nearby tree, maneuvered into a sitting position with her back against the trunk and began moving her hands up and down over the rough bark.

She'd do it for several minutes at a stretch, then rest. It was an unnatural movement and her muscles tired easily.

After half an hour, the wolf suddenly rose, his nose pointed in the direction the man had run, and started growling low in his throat.

Rory stopped moving and waited to see if McDermott was coming back.

After a few minutes, the wolf relaxed and lay on the ground again.

Rory went back to scraping the bark.

It took about two hours before one of the ropes snapped, and just a few seconds after that for her to get her hands completely free and then her legs.

With absolute trust, she put her arms around the wolf's neck and hugged him, then took off running in the general direction of where she thought the road was. The wolf stayed with her, a few paces behind, stopping every few hundred feet to look and listen.

Rory didn't know how long she ran, but it seemed like forever. Just when she thought that maybe she was headed in the wrong direction, there was the road. Her car, of course, was nowhere to be found.

She was going to have to walk. That was all there was to it.

And so she started.

It was late afternoon. No traffic passed her for nearly an hour. When she finally heard the whine of an engine in the distance, she planted herself in the middle of the road and waited.

The car with its woman driver stopped a few feet away from her. Rory ran to the open driver's window. It was the same woman who had been at Daniel's cabin. "I need help. Can you drive me to Jake Troyat's house?"

The woman looked at her for a long moment. She knew who Rory was and she knew the Milbournes were being blamed for the fires.

"Please," said Rory.

The woman sighed. "I guess I can't just leave you here. Get in. Jake's is ten or so miles away."

"Thank you!" Rory ran around to the passenger side and got in.

The woman looked at her as she put the car into drive. "Are you here to see Daniel, as well?"

"Yes."

Her lips drew into a tight line.

Rory looked at her profile. "Are you and he good friends?"

"We're friends." She turned her head and looked at Rory. "Given a chance, we could be more."

Rory folded her hands in her lap and looked out the window. She'd have a chance now, she thought.

"Why are you here?" asked the woman.

"I need to speak with Jake about something."

"And then you'll be leaving?"

"Yes."

She nodded as though she approved.

They rode in silence after that until they reached Jake's house. Rory got out of the car, closed the door and then leaned her head in through the window. "Thanks."

The woman didn't respond.

Rory stepped back and she drove away.

Susan came racing out of the house. "Where have you been? We expected you hours ago."

"I ran into a problem. Is Jake here?"

"No. He and Daniel went to look for you."

No sooner had she said the words than the two men drove up in separate cars. Daniel was driving hers.

Rory didn't see the relief that flooded Daniel's expression as soon as he saw that she was safe.

Jake walked quickly to Rory and put his hands on her shoulders. "Are you all right?"

"Yes. I'm fine now."

"What happened? Why did you leave your car parked on the road with the keys in it?"

"Joe McDermott didn't want me to talk to you. He stopped me on my way here, tied me up and took me into the woods."

Daniel took her chin between his thumb and fore-finger and turned her face toward the fading light. "Did he hit you?"

"Yes."

There was a look in Daniel's eyes that told her more clearly than words that Joe McDermott was lucky he wasn't there.

"How did you get away?" asked Susan.

"The wolf. He came out of nowhere and attacked McDermott."

"Was McDermott bitten?" asked Jake.

"Yes, a couple of times."

"Then he'll have to get treated. I'll get the word out."

Susan looked from Rory to Daniel and decided to follow her husband inside and leave the two of them alone.

Rory's eyes moved over Daniel's face, drinking in everything. It had been two days since she'd last seen him, but it felt like years.

His hand fell to his side. "Susan said you had information about the fires."

"And the mining. And payoffs to a congressman and McDermott."

"Your uncle did it?"

"Yes."

"And your cousin?"

"I didn't see anything that would implicate him."

A muscle in his jaw tightened. "Why would you come to us with this?"

"I had to. What my uncle did, regardless of his motive, was horrible. People lost their homes. They could have been killed. He has to be held responsible for his actions."

The two of them looked at each other for a long time.

Rory blinked first. She wanted his arms around her so badly she ached.

Daniel's eyes remained on her even as she walked away from him.

"Did you find any files in my car?"

"I didn't look."

Rory opened the rear door. Her briefcase was still there. She lifted the flap. The files were still in place. She pulled them out and handed them to Daniel. "Jake will be able to use these."

"Thank you," said Daniel as he took them from her.

Their fingers brushed.

Rory's heart hammered beneath her breast. She tried to ignore it. "There isn't anything in there that specifically ties my uncle to the fires, but I think anyone who looks closely at the information can make an appropriate inference."

"What will you do now?"

"Go back to Chicago and look for a new job, I guess."

"You should be able to easily find one."

"I know. I'm not worried about that."

Jake walked quickly out of the house. "I found him. He's at a hospital about sixty miles from here. I called the city police and we're going together to pick him up.''

Rory couldn't hide her relief. She really believed the man intended to kill her.

''I'll need you to make a statement,'' said Jake to Rory as he climbed into his car. ''And if there's a trial, well, you know the drill.''

She nodded.

Jake took off and Rory was left with Daniel.

He suddenly stepped forward and pulled her into his arms.

Rory held him tightly and buried her face in his shoulder.

Susan was standing on the porch watching them. When she saw the pain on Daniel's face, she turned away in tears and went into the house.

Daniel held Rory away from him and looked into her eyes. ''Take care of yourself.''

She nodded.

''And thank you for this,'' he said, indicating the files.

Rory strove for some sense of normalcy. ''I'm so sorry about everything. How many homes were lost?''

''Seventeen.''

''How will you rebuild?''

''We'll help one another.''

''And the clinic?''

''That's going to require money. I don't know what we're going to do about that yet. For now, I go from house to house.''

''I see.''

An awkward silence fell between them.

Rory shook her head. "Look, I have to go. Say goodbye to Susan for me."

"Of course."

"And tell Jake that I'll keep in touch."

He nodded.

Rory climbed into her car and started the engine. She sat there looking at Daniel, permanently engraving his image on her mind.

There was an ache in her chest like nothing she'd ever felt before. So this was what a broken heart felt like.

She looked away from Daniel and drove off.

Daniel went in search of his grandfather and found him where he knew he would, in the sacred hills. He sat beside him and looked out at the vast expanse of night sky dotted with stars.

The old man turned his head and looked at his grandson. "She's gone?"

Daniel nodded.

"Your Rory has a brave heart to do what she did."

"I know."

"And still you let her go."

Daniel was silent for a long time. "You didn't tell me it would end this way."

Gray Cloud gazed at the sky. "I told you that there would come a time when you would have to make difficult choices. This is one of those choices. And it was the right one, for now. You have a lot of work ahead of you because of the things her family did."

Daniel knew he was right.

"The dishonor may belong to her uncle, but she was here as her uncle's representative," Gray Cloud said.

"I don't think anyone is more acutely aware of that fact than Rory herself.

"I agree with you. And yet . . ."

Daniel knew what his grandfather was trying to say. He'd known it before he'd come to the hills.

He just wanted to ease some of the pain that was like a tearing of his heart.

Now he knew that nothing would ease it. The tear would be with him for the rest of his days.

Chapter Fourteen

Rory looked at the doctor as though he'd lost his mind. "You can't be serious."

"Oh, but I am. You don't have the flu and you aren't ill. You're going to be a mother in about six months."

"But I can't be pregnant!"

The doctor, about sixty and a little on the world-weary side, finished writing in his file and looked at her through thick glasses. "If this is an immaculate conception, let me know now so I can alert the media."

She'd known him since she was a child. In fact, he'd known both of her parents. "It was just one time...."

"That's all it takes, dear." He patted her hand. "Are you all right with this?"

"I don't know. It's such . . ."

"A surprise. I understand. Is the father still in your life?"

"No. Not at all."

He sat in his wheeled chair and looked up at her on the examining table. "You have options."

It took her a moment to understand what he was saying. "Oh, no! I want this baby. There's no question about that."

"It's tough to raise a family alone these days."

She nodded.

"All right." He scribbled something on a piece of paper and handed it to her. "This is the name of an obstetrician-gynecologist I've sent some other patients to her with good results. She's a very good doctor, and I think the two of you will hit it off."

Rory took the paper. "Thank you." She slid off the table.

"Call her right away. You need to have both you and the baby checked out."

"I will."

He looked at her closely. "Are you sure you're all right?"

Rory looked at him for a moment and smiled. "Yes." Then with more force, she added, "Yes! I'm fine. Really fine."

Instead of going back to the law office where she'd worked for the past two months, she went home, put on a robe and lay on the couch. With just the briefest of hesitations, she placed her hand on her still fairly flat stomach. Her baby was there.

Daniel's child.

She looked down and smiled. "We're going to be fine, you and I. I'll be a good mother. And your father..."

She left the thought hanging. There wasn't a day that went by when she didn't think of Daniel and wonder what he was doing. She kept thinking that the pain of not being with him would fade.

It didn't.

How could a man she'd known for such a short time have this kind of effect on her?

Because, she thought, it was Daniel, and he wasn't like any other man.

It was an easy pregnancy except for the first few weeks of morning sickness. After that, she grew ravenously hungry for every kind of food she normally avoided. After a gentle scolding by her doctor, she tried to impose some discipline on herself, but every once in a while, a slice of double fudge cake would force itself on her.

Six months into her pregnancy, she had gained twenty pounds. There was no hiding her condition and she didn't try. The law firm she worked for couldn't have been more supportive.

She was sitting in her eleventh-floor office one day getting ready for a trial the following week when her secretary buzzed her.

"There's a Jake Troyat on the phone for you."

Rory was so surprised that it was a moment before she spoke. "Jake?"

"Yes. He says that he's a friend of yours."

"He is. I just...would you take a message?"

"Sure."

"Wait! Never mind. I'll talk to him."

Rory took a deep breath then punched the button on her speakerphone. "Hello, Jake."

"Hi, kid. How are you doing?"

"Just fine. And you?"

"Never better. Susan asked to be remembered to you."

"Tell her I said hello."

"I will, of course. I hope I'm not catching you at a bad time."

"Not at all."

"I need for you to come to the reservation to give a deposition about Joe McDermott and what happened the day he abducted you."

Rory looked at her bulging stomach. She didn't want Jake to know. "I'm really sorry, Jake, but I can't. I'm in the middle of a lot of work right now."

"Then we'll come to you."

"No, no, that wouldn't be good, either."

There was a pause. "Is everything all right with you?" he asked in concern.

"Yes, of course. I already told you I was fine. I'm just very busy these days."

"It should only take a few hours."

Rory felt cornered. She knew that if she didn't co-operate she could be subpoenaed. At least if she gave the deposition in Chicago, she'd have some control over the circumstances. "When did you have in mind?"

"Next week, on Wednesday. I was thinking early afternoon. How's that for you?"

Rory looked at her calendar. "I'm busy in the morning, but the afternoon looks good. I have a few things I can shuffle off to other attorneys or reschedule."

"Good. Can we use your office?"

"Sure. I'll make sure there's a meeting room available."

"I'll see you Wednesday."

"Jake?"

"What?"

"How are things there? Have people been able to rebuild?"

"Most have, with help from their neighbors. Daniel's still working on his."

Rory cleared her throat. "Daniel. How is he?"

"He's all right." Jake chose his words carefully. "He's the one who organized most of the rebuilding."

"And the clinic?"

"The building is up. Daniel's done some fundraising to buy new equipment, but a lot more is needed."

"I imagine Doris is a lot of help.

"As always."

"And how is Gray Cloud?"

"Like a man half his age."

Rory smiled at the thought. "Would you please give him my regards?"

"Of course. Have you had any contact with your uncle or cousin?"

"Neither of them will speak to me. I can't really blame them. I am, after all, the mother of their predicament."

"I'm sorry."

"Don't be. I don't have any regrets."

"Good girl. I'll see you next week."

"Bye, Jake."

As she punched the button to hang up, she leaned back in her chair and steepled her fingers under her chin. What was she going to do about Jake? If he were to find out she was pregnant, would she be able to trust him not to tell Daniel?

And it was important to her that he not know. Daniel was an honorable man—almost to a fault. She didn't want him to let her back into his life out of a sense of obligation. It was easier to be alone than to have him with her because he felt honor bound.

Her secretary poked her head around the door. "Are you staying late this evening?"

"Until six."

"Do you want me to stay?"

"No, thanks," she said with a smile. "Have a nice evening."

"Believe me, I intend to."

"Big date?"

"Very big."

"Anyone I know?"

"He's only one of our wealthiest clients."

"Harry Taylor?" Rory asked, somewhat surprised.

"The one and only."

"He's too old for you."

"Then you go out with him. He's asked you enough times."

"He's too old for me."

"Mr. Taylor doesn't seem to think so."

"Mr. Taylor would date junior high school girls if it were legal."

"You're so cynical."

Rory shook her head. "You're the one who's going out with him."

She shrugged, then came the rest of the way into the office. "You know, you may be pregnant, but you're still pretty. Why don't you ever go out with the men who ask you?"

"I have other things to concentrate on."

"You'd have fun."

"Maybe after the baby I'll start dating."

Her secretary smiled at her. She and Rory were about the same age, but sometimes Rory seemed so much older. One of these days she was going to take her boss in hand and show her how to have a good time.

The week passed all too quickly. Rory tried on every outfit in her closet, but nothing could hide her condition. There was no way around it. Jake was going to

have to know and she was going to have to trust him
not to tell Daniel.

When he showed up at her office, Rory greeted him
from behind her desk. Jake was wearing his usual
friendly smile. But as she rose to hug him, his eyes
went straight to her stomach and his smile faded.
"What's this?"

"A baby."

He looked into her eyes. "Daniel's?"

"Yes."

He dragged his hand through his hair, clearly upset. "Why haven't you told him?"

"I have my reasons."

"I'm sure you do, but none of them can possibly be
good enough for you to keep this kind of information
away from him. He has a right to know."

"Please, Jake. I don't want to burden him with this.
I chose to have the baby and I'll take care of it."

Jake put his hands on her shoulders. "I don't know
what you're thinking, but he doesn't hold what your
uncle did against you."

"Sure he does. He might not say so directly, but it's
there."

"You're underestimating him."

"You think so? Then why isn't he here?"

"He doesn't know about the baby."

"I don't want him to come here because of a sense
of responsibility toward the baby. I want him to come
here because he loves me. Do you understand?"

"I think you're wrong but, yes, I understand what
you're saying."

"So you won't tell him?"

He sighed. "Not if you don't want me to."

"Thank you."

"May I tell Susan?"

"If you think she can resist telling Daniel."

"It'll be hard for her, but if it's what you want, she can do it." He inclined his head toward her stomach. "When are you due?"

"Eleven weeks."

"Are you scared?"

"Terrified."

Jake walked around the desk and hugged her. "If you need anything, anything at all, you know we're just a phone call away."

She nodded.

He leaned back and gave her the once-over. "You look beautiful."

"I look huge."

"Oh, no," he said with a grin as he shook his head, "I'm not going down that road."

"Smart man."

"You learn these things when you're married."

Rory's smile faded. "You don't have to answer this if you don't want to, but has Daniel been seeing anyone?"

"No. Not since you left."

"It's not really any of my business. I just can't help being curious."

"You're in love with him, aren't you?"

She didn't have to think about it. "Yes."

He sighed. "Well, you already know what I think." He took her by the hand. "Come on. Let's get that deposition taken. And then you and I are going out for a nice dinner."

Chapter Fifteen

Daniel shot straight up in bed. He was out of breath and drenched in perspiration.

He dragged his fingers through his hair. It was Rory. Something was wrong. He got out of bed and, even though it was the middle of the night, he called the Troyats.

Jake answered, his voice thick with sleep.

"I need Rory's phone number."

Jake snapped awake. "Why?"

"Something's wrong. I can feel it. I have to call her to make sure she's all right."

Jake looked across the bed at Susan and covered the mouthpiece with his hand. "It's Daniel. He wants Rory's phone number."

"Give it to him," she whispered back.

"He thinks something's wrong," he whispered.

Susan looked at her husband for a long moment. "It's time. I bet she's having the baby."

"Jake, give me the number," said Daniel.

Jake wanted to tell him so badly his wife could see it in his expression. But Susan knew her husband well. He would never be able to betray a trust.

Susan, on the other hand, had no such problem. At least not with this. If ever there was a time for common sense, this was it. She took the phone from Jake. "Daniel, Rory's probably in labor."

There was a long pause. "What?"

"She's pregnant with your child. Jake and I wanted to tell you, but we gave her our word that we wouldn't."

"Where is she?"

"We know where she lives, but we don't know what hospital—if in fact that's what's going on. It would probably be one close to her apartment."

"I've got to get there."

Jake took the phone from his wife. "There aren't any commuter flights this late at night. I think the fastest thing would be for you to drive there. You get ready to go and I'll make a few phone calls to see if I can locate her. Don't leave until you hear from me."

"Jake, you should have told me."

"I'm sorry. I couldn't. But since you know now, the least I can do is find out where she is. I'll call you right back."

* * *

Rory was in one of the homey labor rooms of her hospital. She had just finished having a painful contraction.

She was exhausted but couldn't sleep. Every time she started to doze off, she got hit with another contraction. She wanted to have natural childbirth without drugs but, in all honesty, painkillers were sounding better all the time.

She looked around the room that had been her home for the past fifteen hours. There was delicately flowered wallpaper with matching chintz drapes. Instead of the usual hospital furniture, there was a couch and an easy chair.

She looked at the monitor next to her bed. It seemed to know when she was going to have a contraction before she did.

And there it was.

She did her best Lamaze breathing, just the way she'd been taught, but it still hurt like hell. Tears slid from the corners of her eyes when it was over.

A nurse came in and smiled sympathetically. "It's not much fun, is it?"

Rory didn't answer.

While the nurse checked the different monitors, Rory dozed off without even realizing it.

It was just a few minutes later when she had another contraction. She groaned and opened her eyes as the pain grew more intense.

Daniel was there.

Or maybe she'd just imagined him.

His hand stroked her damp hair. "It's going to be okay, Rory," he said. "Breathe."

Breathing was just about all she could do. How could anyone be in this much pain and live?

The contraction eased.

And Daniel was still there. She hadn't imagined him. "What are you doing here?" she asked.

He looked into her teary eyes. "I came to do what I can to help the woman I love deliver my child."

"How did you know?"

"I always know when something happens to you."

"You're not making any sense."

"I've carried you in my heart since the moment you were born," he said. "I knew something had happened to you when your parents died, and I knew something was happening to you tonight. The difference tonight is that I knew where to find you."

"How could you know when I was born, or that we'd ever meet?"

"My grandfather saw it all."

Some of Gray Cloud's odd remarks suddenly made sense. Like when she'd asked him if Daniel had told him about her and he'd said that, on the contrary, he'd been the one who'd told Daniel. "Are you here right now because of the baby?"

"I'm here because of you."

There was another contraction. Daniel helped her concentrate on her breathing.

"How long have you been in labor?" he asked when it was over.

"Too long. I don't know. I couldn't even tell you what time it is at the moment."

"I'll be right back. I want to talk to one of the nurses."

Rory closed her eyes. When she opened them again, Daniel was back.

He moved from the chair to the edge of the bed and gently pushed her hair away from her face. "Have I ever told you how much I like your curls?"

"They're a curse. No one takes a person with hair like this seriously." She looked into his warm brown eyes. "Why did you send me away?"

"Because it was the only thing I could do at the time. I knew you'd be safer in Chicago. And I thought you'd probably be better off without me."

"How could you have thought that?"

"Rory, I live on a reservation in a cabin. I'm a doctor who earns very little money. I have nothing to offer you."

"I don't want anything except you. I loved the cabin because you were there. And I could never mind not having money as long as I was with you. Didn't you know that?"

His eyes moved over her face. "I guess not."

She had another contraction. This one had to have been off the scale. Rory was sure she was going to die in the middle of it. "I can't do this anymore," she gasped when it was over.

Daniel held her hand. "It won't be long now."

"Is that what the nurse said?"

"Yes."

There was another one.

Her doctor walked into the room with a smile. "How's the almost-new mother doing?" she asked.

"Do you remember when we talked about this and I told you I didn't want any drugs?"

"Yes."

"I've changed my mind."

The doctor checked to see how dilated Rory was. "Too late, my dear. The newest member of your family is ready to make his or her appearance."

Rory looked up at Daniel. He smiled at her and squeezed her hand.

"Are you the father?" asked the doctor.

"Yes."

"Ask the nurse for a sterile gown and gloves. We're going to the delivery room."

Daniel and the doctor left while a nurse came in, detached the two monitors Rory was hooked up to, raised the sides of the bed and wheeled her out.

There was another contraction.

"Keep breathing," said the nurse. "Don't push yet. Not until the doctor tells you to."

"I have to."

"No, you don't. Just keep breathing."

As soon as they were in the delivery room, the doctor took a seat right in front of Rory's propped-up legs. Daniel entered a moment later and took Rory's hand in his. "It's almost over," he said.

There was another contraction.

"Okay, Rory," said her doctor, "do what comes naturally and start pushing."

She pushed.

And pushed.

And pushed.

"We're almost there," said the doctor. "Come on. Push a little harder."

There was a piercing pain when the baby's shoulders came through and then, like that, it was over.

The baby gave a lusty cry as soon as he made his entrance into the world. "You have," said the doctor, "a perfect baby boy. Congratulations."

Daniel leaned over and kissed Rory tenderly on the lips.

She raised her hand to his face. "I'm so glad you came."

A nurse laid the baby on Rory's chest while the doctor finished her work. He was beautiful, with a shock of hair every bit as black as his father's.

"He looks like you," said Rory.

Daniel lifted his son's tiny hand and gazed at it in wonder. He'd delivered babies at the clinic. They were all miracles. But no miracle had ever touched him like the birth of his own son. "Have you decided on a name?" he asked.

"Sam."

"Sam," repeated Daniel. "I like it. It suits him."

The nurse took the baby. "I'll just clean him up a little and bring him right back."

Daniel, full of emotion, leaned over Rory and placed his cheek against hers. "I love you beyond words," he said in a soft whisper only she could hear.

Rory couldn't imagine a moment happier than this. She had been so sure that Daniel was out of her life forever. But now he was here. He'd helped her bring their son into the world.

And he loved her.

Epilogue

Rory stood quietly smiling in the doorway of the cabin Daniel had spent the past two years rebuilding. It was larger than the one that had burned down. There was still an open kitchen and main room, but now there were also two bedrooms.

The scene outside warmed her heart. Gray Cloud was sitting on the ground with his almost-two-year-old great-grandson, explaining the intricacies of nature and man's connection to it. The two of them spent hours together every day. Sam adored his great-grandfather and his great-grandfather clearly adored him. The wolf sat nearby, his head on his paws, but alert, his eyes missing nothing.

Daniel came up behind her, wrapped her in his arms and pulled her back against his chest as he nuzzled her hair.

Rory melted, as she did every time her husband touched her, turned her head and rubbed her cheek against his chest.

"What are you thinking?" he asked.

"How lucky I am."

Daniel looked at his son and smiled. The little boy had long, dark hair, like his father. But his eyes were the same remarkable blue color as his mother's. He was a beautiful boy, tall for his age and straight, usually serious, with an occasional mischievous twinkle. And he was secure in the love that surrounded him.

"Are you working at home today?" asked Daniel.

Rory had opened her own small law office in town, but she did most of her work at home so she could stay with Sam. "Yes."

"I wish I could stay here with you."

"Ah, but the clinic awaits."

Daniel turned her in his arms and lowered his mouth to hers, kissing her so deeply she could feel it to her core. Her response was instant and passionate.

Daniel groaned as he raised his head and looked into her eyes. "I love you."

She smiled as she rose on tiptoe and kissed the corner of his mouth. "You want me."

"I always want you."

As she pulled her body close to his, she knew it was true.

Daniel pushed her curls away from her face and his expression grew serious. "Do you ever regret anything that's happened?"

Her smile faded as she thought about his question. "I wouldn't call it regret. I'm saddened at times by what I did to my uncle, and I'm sorry to have lost him, but I don't regret it."

"What about leaving Chicago and turning your life completely upside down for me?"

"Oh, no," she said softly. She touched his cheek with gentle fingertips. "No. I've never been happier than I am here with you and Sam. When I thought I'd lost you for good, it was all I could do to get myself through a day. Even when I was pregnant, I felt as though a part of me were missing—the part of me that was you. I could never be whole as long as you were gone from my life."

Daniel pulled her into his arms and held her. "You've haunted me every moment of my life since you were born. It was hell when I was old enough to understand what it meant. I looked for you in every woman I met. And then you showed up here. A Milbourne."

Rory sighed against his chest. "I love you, Daniel."

He held her more tightly. "I can't imagine my life without you in it."

"You don't have to. I'm here and I'm not going anywhere."

Sam came running in and wrapped one arm around Rory's leg and one around Daniel's. The two of them looked at each other and smiled, then looked at the beautiful child they'd created.

If there was such a thing as perfect happiness, this was it.

* * * * *

MILLION DOLLAR SWEEPSTAKES (III)

No purchase necessary. To enter, follow the directions published. Method of entry may vary. For eligibility, entries must be received no later than March 31, 1996. No liability is assumed for printing errors, lost, late or misdirected entries. Odds of winning are determined by the number of eligible entries distributed and received. Prizewinners will be determined no later than June 30, 1996.

Sweepstakes open to residents of the U.S. (except Puerto Rico), Canada, Europe and Taiwan who are 18 years of age or older. All applicable laws and regulations apply. Sweepstakes offer void wherever prohibited by law. Values of all prizes are in U.S. currency. This sweepstakes is presented by Torstar Corp., its subsidiaries and affiliates, in conjunction with book, merchandise and/or product offerings. For a copy of the Official Rules send a self-addressed, stamped envelope (WA residents need not affix return postage) to: MILLION DOLLAR SWEEPSTAKES (III) Rules, P.O. Box 4573, Blair, NE 68009, USA.

EXTRA BONUS PRIZE DRAWING

No purchase necessary. The Extra Bonus Prize will be awarded in a random drawing to be conducted no later than 5/30/96 from among all entries received. To qualify, entries must be received by 3/31/96 and comply with published directions. Drawing open to residents of the U.S. (except Puerto Rico), Canada, Europe and Taiwan who are 18 years of age or older. All applicable laws and regulations apply; offer void wherever prohibited by law. Odds of winning are dependent upon number of eligibile entries received. Prize is valued in U.S. currency. The offer is presented by Torstar Corp., its subsidiaries and affiliates in conjunction with book, merchandise and/or product offering. For a copy of the Official Rules governing this sweepstakes, send a self-addressed, stamped envelope (WA residents need not affix return postage) to: Extra Bonus Prize Drawing Rules, P.O. Box 4590, Blair, NE 68009, USA.

SWP-S1195

**Who needs mistletoe when
Santa's Little Helpers are around?**

Santa's Little Helpers

brought to you by:

Janet Dailey
Jennifer Greene
Patricia Gardner Evans

This holiday collection has three contemporary stories
celebrating the joy of love during Christmas.
Featuring a BRAND-NEW story from *New York Times*
bestselling author Janet Dailey, this special anthology
makes the perfect holiday gift for you or a loved one!

FREE GIFT
with purchase
see inside

You can receive a beautiful 18" goldtone rope
necklace—absolutely FREE—with the purchase of
Santa's Little Helpers. See inside the book for details.
Santa's Little Helpers—a holiday gift you will want
to open again and again!

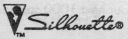

Silhouette®